"So, Betsy Ames didn't do badly for herself after all."

Grady reached for her left hand, holding it up to admire the broad gold band on her ring finger. "When you couln't catch one of the heirs of Logan Banks in your attractively baited trap, you settled for the heir of the Englin Hotels. Not bad for a girl who used to be a hotel maid."

Elizabeth yanked her hand away. "In case you don't remember, it wasn't me who was chasing you!"

"Come off it, Betsy. You were flirting with me from the moment I arrived at that awful little inn."

"It didn't seem to bother you at the time. And you didn't waste any time making plans for the future when you ran out on me."

"I was called back to New York," Grady corrected. "And a few days without you let me get my perspective back...."

"And you started thanking your guardian angel that you hadn't made any permanent arrangements."

"Right. And I've been thanking him ever since, you little gold digger."

Dear Reader,

This month we celebrate the publication of our 1000th Harlequin Presents. It is a special occasion for us, and one we would like to share with you.

Since its inception with three of our bestselling authors in May, 1973, Harlequin Presents has grown to become the most popular romance series in the world, featuring more than sixty internationally acclaimed authors. All of the authors appearing this month are well-known and loved. Some have been with us right from the start; others are newer, but each, in the tradition of Harlequin Presents, delivers the passionate exciting love stories our readers have come to expect.

We are proud of the trust you have placed in us over the years. It's part of the Harlequin dedication to supplying, contemporary fiction, rich in romance, exotic settings and happy endings.

We know you'll enjoy all of the selections in this very special month, and in the months to come.

Your friends at Harlequin

LEIGH MICHAELS

the grand hotel

Harlequin Books

TORONTO • NEW YORK • LONDON
AMSTERDAM • PARIS • SYDNEY • HAMBURG
STOCKHOLM • ATHENS • TOKYO • MILAN

For Michael
—who believed in me—
with all my love

Harlequin Presents first edition August 1987
ISBN 0-373-11004-9

Original hardcover edition published in 1983
by Mills & Boon Limited

CHAPTER ONE

As Elizabeth parked her car in the guest drive of the Englin Hotel, she noticed that the canopy over the bank of revolving doors was beginning to fray at the edges. The cream-coloured trim on the deep maroon was suffering from the weather. She made a mental note to mention it to the maintenance department.

The doorman, in his maroon livery, let a smile cross his usually impassive face as he opened her car door. 'It's good to see you back, Mrs Englin,' he said cheerfully.

Elizabeth reached for her handbag and stepped out of the car, her skirt sliding up elegant long legs. 'Henry, I've only been gone since Friday,' she chided.

'It seems longer,' he said. 'Shall I have the boys park your car and bring up your bags?'

'Please.' She handed him the keys to the dark-green Porsche. 'Everything running smoothly?' The person she should have addressed the question to was the assistant manager on duty, but Henry had been at the Englin as long as Elizabeth could remember. The assistant manager might be the proper person to answer the question, but Henry had the feel of the great hotel. If anything was not running smoothly, Henry always knew it.

'There have been a few snags. Nothing major.' Henry motioned to a bellboy.

Elizabeth smiled and went on into the hotel lobby.

She stood on the stylised 'E' woven into the centre of the maroon carpet under the silver chandelier and took a deep breath. The air held the faint fragrance that she had always associated with the Englin—a mixture of furniture wax, wood smoke, and freshly ground coffee mixed with a multitude of other scents Elizabeth had never been able to isolate. Again today, as she had throughout her five years as general manager of the hotel, she gave up, and ruefully shook her head as she walked through the lobby to the registration desk.

At the assistant manager's desk, a dark-haired girl in the tailored maroon jacket of an assistant manager looked up with a blinding smile. 'Welcome home, Mrs Englin,' she said.

'Hi, Jill. Are you on duty this weekend?'

'No, I have one more week of training left. Mr Bradford is on duty. He's up in one of the penthouse suites taking care of details: it was rented this afternoon.'

Elizabeth noted with interest the way Jill said her supervisor's name. So she thought Tom Bradford was pretty special, did she? Well, he was an unusual person; that was why he was Elizabeth's chief assistant. 'Whenever he's free, tell him I'm back. I'll be in my apartment the rest of the day if there's anything important.' Tom Bradford was good at his job; he was certainly as capable as she of catering to almost any of the people who rented the Englin's penthouse suites. 'It wasn't the President of the United States, was it?' she asked Jill, almost as an afterthought.

Jill grinned. 'No. At least, there aren't any Secret Servicemen around.'

'Then Mr Bradford doesn't need me,' Elizabeth said. Besides, she told herself, it was Sunday afternoon. Surely she was entitled to finish her weekend off. With Henry and Jill both aware of her return, the grapevine would be working overtime. No doubt Tom Bradford, up on the top floor, had already been told she was back. She smiled ruefully. Trying to sneak up on an employee at the Englin to observe his job performance was downright impossible.

She walked back into the big lobby. She wasn't ready to

go up to the apartment yet, and she wasn't ready to go back to work. She just wanted a few minutes to reabsorb the atmosphere of the Englin. She forgot how much the hotel meant to her until she went away for a few days. She stopped in front of the huge fireplace, the marble rubbed to a gleam. The fire was laid, ready to be lit if the evening was cool. It probably wouldn't be, even with the breeze coming off the lake-front, because it was August. But the fires were always ready.

It had been a weekend that brought back memories better left buried, she told herself, and wondered if she had been utterly stupid to go back to that little town in Wisconsin. She hadn't been there in five years, and she had been trying to exorcise a ghost by going back. Maybe if she saw the inn again, she had thought, she could get those memories uprooted and dispose of them as casually as she would discard last year's clothes. It hadn't worked that way, of course. If anything, the memories were stronger now. The little inn in Bridgedale had burned down years ago, and a factory now occupied the site. But the memories remained. In her mind, she supposed, it would always be summer in Bridgedale.

She sighed and walked slowly to the elevators. The express whisked her to the twenty-third floor, just one floor below the penthouses. There was a bit of bright-coloured chintz fabric pulled loose inside the lift; Elizabeth added it to her mental list to talk to the maintenance department about. A luxury hotel charging luxury prices could not afford to look shabby in the least detail, especially when old-fashioned elegance was the strongest attraction to the patrons.

She let herself into the apartment with her key and sighed in relief when she saw the closed door of Myles' study. She wasn't capable of facing him right now; it would be hard enough to put on a good face for Florence, the housekeeper. She went down the hall to the kitchen.

Florence looked up as she came in. 'Heard you were back,' she said laconically.

'The Englin's grapevine never fails,' Elizabeth said wryly, selecting a radish from the tray Florence was arranging. 'Is Myles watching the baseball game on TV?'

'No. He has a guest.'

'Oh.' Elizabeth sat down on a stool at the breakfast bar. 'I can think of things I'd rather do tonight than entertain. Or is it a stag party?' Her tone was hopeful.

Florence shook her head. 'He was asking just a few minutes ago if you were home yet. Said to tell you to dress casually.'

'Ha! Myles doesn't know what the word means. Someday I'm going to take him literally and show up in blue jeans.'

'I wouldn't do it tonight.' Florence put a tray of *hors d'oeuvres* in the oven. 'And I didn't know you owned any jeans.'

'Figuratively speaking, of course. Whom do we have the honour of entertaining?'

'I never saw the guy before. He's a banker. Name's Logan.' She began to slice celery.

Elizabeth's hand clenched on the edge of the counter, the broad gold band on the ring finger cutting into her flesh. Then she forced herself to relax. 'You were on vacation last time he was here. He's an old friend of Myles', but they don't see each other very often. Filthy rich.'

'Going after him?'

'Are you kidding? Whit Logan is extremely married.'

Florence shrugged. 'Just an idea.'

'Well, get rid of it. I'm not in the market for a husband.'

'Maybe you should be, Elizabeth.'

'Florence, it's none of your business.'

Another shrug, but Florence changed the subject. 'How did Jeremy like being left in Wisconsin?'

Elizabeth selected another radish. 'He was out of the car before I could get it stopped, and from then on all I saw of Jeremy was a blur in the distance. He loves the country so much. I think he'd be delighted if we'd move up there.'

'How long did you tell me he's staying?'

'Tonya's coming home this weekend so she has a couple of weeks to get Brian ready to start school. A week with two five-year-olds, and she'll be ready for a break.'

The housekeeper eyed Elizabeth for a moment. 'Tonya will take good care of him.'

'I know she will. It's just that I said goodbye to him only four hours ago, and I'm already feeling lonely.'

Florence nodded. 'It's good for him, though. He's too dependent on you. He needs a father, Elizabeth.'

'Florence, for the last time—' Words failed Elizabeth and she stalked out of the room. Chances were, if she had still been in the kitchen when her voice came back, she would have said something she'd really regret.

Instinct and mother-longing made her go into Jeremy's room. It was unnaturally neat now; Florence must have cleaned it as soon as they had left on Friday. Usually Jeremy's floor was populated with miniature soldiers, game pieces, and scraps of paper on which he was design- ing unknown new machinery. Like all five-year-olds, he thoroughly enjoyed clutter. The room didn't look right with the bedspread pulled up straight and even, and the pillow flat instead of punched up into a wad.

She had said goodbye to him just hours before; surely she wasn't such a clinging vine of a mother to be homesick for her son so quickly. Elizabeth prided herself on her independence, and she was trying to raise Jeremy to be self-sufficient, too. Florence was wrong when she said the child was dependent; yet it hurt Elizabeth when he didn't seem to mind at all that he wouldn't see her for a week.

'It's because you're a mother, dummy,' she told herself

sternly. 'And all mothers are known to go slightly bananas when their offspring start to grow up.' If you think you're bad now, she added silently, wait till he comes back and starts to go to school. That will really throw your mind into a spin.

She sat down in the bentwood rocker she had used to rock him to sleep as an infant. Now, more often than not, the chair was his rocket to the stars, or his cow pony, or his fire engine.

Elizabeth absently turned the gold ring on her left hand. Was Florence right? Was Jeremy missing something vital because there were just the two of them? Myles loved the boy, but he was just too old to be much of a father figure. Especially since his last heart attack, his activity had been strictly limited, and Jeremy's boundless energy wore him out. Much of the time, he just didn't want to be bothered.

She suddenly became aware of the nervous habit of turning the ring endlessly, and stopped, remembering Jeremy's father. Would that frozen spot in her heart ever thaw? Would she ever be able to remember him without the sharp agony of loss?

'It's been years,' she told herself firmly. Was Florence right? Should she think of marriage, for Jeremy's sake?

The answer came so quickly that she knew it was the right one. No. There were things that even the most loving mother would not do for her child. Marriage was one of them.

She picked up the shaker of goldfish food and fed the calico and the fantail which were swimming aimlessly around the aquarium. It was pure fancy to think that they missed Jeremy already, too, she told herself.

Florence had even removed the baseball cap which usually hung from the mirror on Jeremy's dresser. Feeling a little foolish, Elizabeth hunted in the closet until she found it, and put it on the mirror at Jeremy's favourite angle. It seemed a promise to herself that the week would be shorter than she expected, and on Friday her boy would be home again.

Elizabeth detoured into the kitchen on her way to the big living room. 'How do I look?' she asked Florence.

'Turn round.'

Elizabeth obediently turned, the full skirt of the hostess dress whispering around her ankles. The dress was a tiny sprigged print of dark green on cream, the green the same shade as Elizabeth's eyes. Her flaxen hair, the palest of golds, was arranged in a knot on top of her head. Her entire appearance, precisely what Myles would call casual, would not have been out of place at any night-club in the city.

'Nice,' Florence said. 'Where did you buy that dress?'

'The bargain basement at Marshall Field,' Elizabeth teased.

'It's good to see the sparkle back in your eyes.'

'I was just feeling a little silly about Jeremy being gone.'

'You do that every time he leaves the building.'

Elizabeth reached for a cracker. 'Then I shouldn't worry about it any more, should I?'

'No. Want to make yourself useful? Take in the appetisers.' Florence pushed a silver and crystal tiered tray across the counter.

'All right. When will dinner be ready?'

'Half an hour.'

'Do you suppose if this turns into a dead bore, I could develop a headache?'

'It might fool Mr Logan. But you could surely come up with a better excuse for Mr Englin.'

'I'll work on it.'

Myles Englin was sitting in his favourite chair, and as she came into the room Elizabeth had eyes only for him. But his colour was good, and he was smiling, and she breathed a quick sigh of relief. Whenever she left him, she was uncertain of what she would find on her return, especially since that last attack. She dropped a kiss on his cheek. 'Would you like something to nibble on?' she asked. 'Florence said dinner will be in half an hour.'

He took a tiny patty shell. 'It's good to have you home, Elizabeth,' he said. 'You wouldn't believe how lonely this place is without you.'

'With baseball season reaching fever pitch, you were probably so involved you didn't even miss me,' she teased.

'Shows how much attention you pay to baseball, dear. The Cubs aren't even close to a pennant. How can I get excited when my team is back in the pack? I'd like you to meet my guest. You remember Whit Logan, don't you?'

'Of course,' Elizabeth said, and raised her head, for the first time looking at the man who had been pouring himself a drink, his back turned, when she came into the room. But this wasn't Whit Logan . . . that thick dark hair, those square broad shoulders could never have belonged to Whit Logan. . .

'This is Whit's son Grady; Grady, my granddaughter, Elizabeth Englin.'

With a smile that hurt her mouth, Elizabeth extended her hand. 'Mr Logan,' she said. Her voice, to her own ears, sounded strained and cracked. 'We enjoyed having your father visit us when he was in town a few months ago.'

Grady Logan took her hand and held it for an instant, dropping it so quickly it was an insult. His sapphire-blue eyes met her green ones, and Elizabeth didn't flinch. In that split second she had regained her poise, learned well in five years of managing the hotel; not by the flicker of an eyelash did she betray her emotions as she moved to the bar and poured herself a glass of wine.

'May I call you Elizabeth? Or do you prefer something less formal—Betsy, for example?' The blue eyes were hard. Grady Logan took a long drink of his Scotch.

Elizabeth forced a laugh. So the gloves are off, and the knives are coming out, she thought. 'Elizabeth will be fine, Mr Logan. Or may I call you Grady? What brings you to Chicago?'

'I'm a vice-president of my father's company now. I'll be making Chicago my headquarters while I supervise all of the Logan banks in this part of the country.'

Elizabeth speared an appetiser on a toothpick. 'You must be very attached to your father,' she said sweetly.

Grady's jaw set, and Elizabeth knew that her jibe had struck home. It would indeed be comfortable to be the son of Whit Logan. At least one would always have a job—as long as one did what Daddy told you to, she added to herself. And if one didn't obey ... Grady might be a vice-president now, but she was willing to bet that the senior Mr Logan still made the decisions.

Florence came in to announce dinner just then, and Myles set his glass down. 'You two youngsters lead the way,' he said. 'I'll trail along behind. I've slowed down a lot, you know, Grady. After all, I'm seventy-five now, and not as healthy as I used to be. If I didn't have Elizabeth here, the Englin would have been on the market long ago.'

Grady pulled Elizabeth's hand through the crook of his arm. 'I'm sure you must be very attached to her,' he said dryly.

At the table, Myles poured three glasses of wine, and when Elizabeth murmured a protest, he said, 'Not even my doctor could be upset if I have a little wine to celebrate a happy occasion, Elizabeth.' He raised the glass. 'To our new neighbour,' he said.

Elizabeth nearly choked. What did that mean? she wondered, then immediately assured herself that Myles meant only to welcome Grady to Chicago.

But before she could recover completely, he turned to

her. 'I don't think I mentioned, Elizabeth, that Grady's rented one of the penthouses.'

She murmured something indistinct and raised her wineglass again, remembering now what Jill had said about the penthouse suite being rented that afternoon. Grady Logan living one floor above her? How in God's green earth was she to put up with that? 'I'm sure we'll be delighted to have you until you locate something permanent. Apartments are hard to find just now, but. . .'

Grady's blue eyes bored through her. 'This is permanent, Elizabeth. I signed a year's lease this afternoon.'

'Oh. I thought, of course . . . I'm sorry.'

Myles sent her a sharp look, and Elizabeth stared at her plate, hoping to dull his suspicion. Many of the penthouses were rented on a more or less permanent basis, but most of the tenants used them only infrequently. She should have been delighted that one was rented as a permanent apartment. She had better be careful or Myles would be more than just suspicious.

'I'm sure you'll be happy there, Grady,' Myles said. 'The Maxwell is a beautiful apartment.'

It would have to be the Maxwell that he'd rented, Elizabeth told herself bitterly. The Maxwell was her favourite, the first of the penthouses to get a full remodelling and decorating. Elizabeth had chosen the colours and furnishings from carpet to chandeliers within the last six months. And now it's first long-term tenant was to be Grady Logan. It was too ironic to bear.

But surely, after finding out that she was here, he would want to break that lease. Elizabeth made a mental note to call the hotel's attorney first thing in the morning. Alan was a good friend as well as a crack lawyer, and he had helped her out of scrapes before. He would be able to tell her what to do. She would make it as easy for Grady as she could. She'd swear he'd had as big a shock there in the drawing room as she had.

Myles spent the rest of the dinner hour telling Grady about Elizabeth's plans to convert all of the larger suites into apartments. He tried to draw her into the conversation, but Elizabeth refused to co-operate.

'It's a brilliant notion, really,' he said. 'With rentals scarce and prices high along the whole lake-shore, plus the newer luxury hotels taking over a lot of the market for big suites, we can settle for a little lower price but end up with a steadier return.'

'Is the Englin still so popular with the celebrities?'

'Are you hoping to run into movie starlets in the elevator?' Elizabeth asked, and immediately regretted it.

Grady answered, 'No,' and his level gaze told Elizabeth that if she didn't want to accept the consequences she had better watch what she said.

Myles said, 'No, they've moved on up the street. At least the younger ones have. We still have some who are faithful. That's one of the reasons you'll find it so peaceful up there. Some of the apartments are empty, waiting to be refurnished, and most of the rest are rented to people who use them only once a year or so.'

'Did you ever think of selling the hotel?'

'Yes. I'd hate to, though we have divested ourselves of the rest of the chain. There were fifteen Englins, you know, in my younger days. They stretched from California to the Caribbean.' He sighed. 'But after my heart attacks, my doctor wouldn't hear of me managing all the places. Elizabeth couldn't handle everything, so we had no choice. But this one was the original Englin, and she loves it as much as I do. No, we won't let go of this one.'

Grady didn't say anything, but Elizabeth could almost hear the cynical bite of the words he was longing to say. She just smiled sweetly at him and wondered what he was going to do with a ten-room apartment. The Maxwell had four bedrooms. Maybe he was planning to move in with a harem. Or maybe Papa Logan had come up with an

approved girl, and Grady was raising a family of miniature bankers. The thought made her stomach ache.

It was hard to reconcile the amiable, though hard-
headed businessman, Whit Logan, who had even conde-
scended to notice Jeremy on his last visit, with the pat-
riarch who kept his son under his thumb. Maybe she had
misread the man when he had visited; heaven knew it was
easy enough to put on a charming face for an evening. Or
perhaps she had overestimated the control he had over
Grady? No, she told herself. There had been no doubt left
about that.

'Elizabeth!' Myles said.

Elizabeth jumped. She had been staring into her coffee
cup, wondering absently if Grady was married and what
his wife was like. She looked up at Myles.

'What's the matter with you tonight, dear? I merely
suggested you take Grady down to the Library Lounge for
an Irish coffee. I know I must be boring you to death,
Grady. Nothing worse than telling a banker all of your
financial plans, unless it's asking a doctor to diagnose
your gall bladder problem at a cocktail party.'

Grady grinned. 'Not at all, Myles. But I couldn't turn
down the Irish coffee.' He reached for Elizabeth's elbow.

'Be sure the waitress puts it on my tab, Elizabeth,'
Myles said. 'Goodnight, now.'

Elizabeth started to protest, but the hand on her arm
tightened warningly. 'All right, all right,' she said, and led
the way out of the apartment.

CHAPTER TWO

In the elevator, Elizabeth shook Grady's hand off her arm. 'This wasn't my idea,' she said defiantly.

'You don't want me to rock the boat, do you? Little Betsy Ames didn't do so badly for herself after all.' He reached for her left hand again, holding it up to admire the broad gold band on her ring finger.

'Would you like to explain that remark?'

'I don't see why I should have to, but if you insist, I will. When you couldn't catch one of the heirs of the Logan banks in your attractively-baited trap, you settled for the heir of the Englin hotels. And ingratiated yourself so far with the old man that when your husband died, you became the favourite. Not bad for a girl who used to be a hotel maid. Tell me, is that how you captivated Rick Englin? The same way you were working on me?'

Elizabeth yanked her hand out of his grip. 'For your information, in case you don't remember, it wasn't me who was chasing you, but the other way around.' So that was what he thought had happened.

'Oh, come off it, Betsy.' He leaned against the brass rail that circled the elevator, one hand pushing his jacket back, fingers tucked in his trouser pocket. 'You were flirting with me from the moment I arrived at that awful little inn.'

'It didn't seem to bother you at the time. And you certainly didn't waste any time making plans for the future when you ran out on me.'

'I was called back to New York,' Grady corrected.

'No doubt because your father's spies had been busy.'

'No doubt.' It didn't seem to bother him. 'If it had been

up to me, I'd have stayed. And I was so besotted I'd probably have proposed to you, and you'd have had all the money and social position you wanted, until my father disowned me. I wonder what you'd have done then.'

'You have all my sympathy.'

'But I was called away, and a few days without you let me get my perspective back. . .'

'And you started thanking your guardian angel that you hadn't made any permanent arrangements.'

'Right. And I've been thanking him ever since, you little gold-digger.' He swept her an elaborate bow. 'I beg your pardon, Mrs Englin.' The tone made the words an insult.

The elevator doors opened. 'I'll say goodnight now, Grady. But there is one question I'd like you to answer. Was it your father who told you the Englin would be a good place to live?'

'Why do you want to know?' He stretched out a hand to keep the elevator door from closing again.

'Because I'd be delighted to write him a note about why it isn't going to work out. Goodnight.'

'Your doting grandfather—you must really have worked the charm on him to reach the stage where he actually considers you part of the family—insisted that we have a drink. I'm sure he's perfectly capable of checking his bar tab to be sure it's listed there.'

'I'll tell him you insisted on paying for it. He'll believe me. He has no reason to think you're not a gentleman.'

'Nevertheless, we're going to finish this discussion in a more private place. Shall it be the Library, or would you prefer my apartment? It doesn't have all of the amenities yet, but it's private.'

Elizabeth glanced around. The lobby was quiet, but one never knew when it would bustle, and she certainly didn't want to go up to the Maxwell. Something told her that if she tried to avoid him, Grady wouldn't hesitate to follow her into her own apartment and say whatever it was he intended to say. 'The Library's to your left, past the registration desk,' she said, resigned.

It was a slack time, and the only clerk at the desk was reading a news magazine. At the assistant manager's desk Tom Bradford was working on arrangements for a convention group that would be arriving the following week. The plans seemed to be bothering him, for he was tugging at his beard in a gesture characteristic of puzzlement. He was working overtime, Elizabeth noted; she wondered why he wasn't upstairs in the office. He looked up in surprise when he saw them, but Elizabeth merely smiled and hurried on past. She supposed she should stop and introduce Grady as the Maxwell's new tenant, in case Tom hadn't already met him, but she was determined that by tomorrow she'd have that lease broken. Why create any waves? Let Tom wonder why she was going into the cocktail lounge on the new tenant's arm. It wasn't any of Tom's business anyway.

Grady had tucked her hand into the crook of his elbow, and he didn't let go until the waitress had led them to a table near the big fireplace with its mantel carved of oak. Behind glass doors a fire crackled, adding charm to the big room.

'Nice little place,' Grady said, leaning back in his chair to study the surroundings. 'Was this your idea, too?'

Grudgingly, Elizabeth replied, 'No. The Library's been a part of the Englin from the beginning.' She too looked up beyond the balcony that marked where the second floor normally would have been, to the upper reaches of the two-storey room where the corners were hidden by a dusk that the indirect lighting was never intended to reach. Books, many of them old and rare, their gold-trimmed bindings gleaming in the light, lent a mellowness to the atmosphere. Above the elaborately-carved mantel hung the family crest, one of the few things saved from the

original Englin Hotel which had stood in the same block
and had been destroyed by the Great Chicago Fire.

'Who are the people in the portraits?' Grady asked,
waving a casual hand towards the massive gold frames
which flanked the fireplace.

Elizabeth looked up at them too. 'My ... Myles'
grandparents, when they were first married.' The waitress
brought their Irish coffee, and Elizabeth signed the tab.
Inhaling the cinnamon fragrance of the brew, she studied
the portraits. 'He built this hotel after the fire destroyed
the original Englin. He'd travelled in Germany and
Bavaria; that's why it looks vaguely like a European
castle.'

'You're big on the family history, aren't you? I'll bet
that you have the Englins traced all the way back to
William the Conqueror. Too bad your own family had no
such illustrious origins.'

Her green eyes summed him up. 'You never used to be
petty,' Elizabeth said finally. 'And any family can pro-
duce a bad apple.'

'Implying that I am one? Don't throw stones,
Betsy.'

She sighed and sipped her coffee. 'If you dragged me in
here to tell me you'd like to break the lease, I understand
perfectly. I'll have our attorney contact you, and I'll even
explain it to Myles somehow.'

'You'd like me to break that lease, wouldn't you,
Betsy?'

'My name is Elizabeth.'

'I understand. It has a lot more class, doesn't it? It goes
much better with your new image.' He picked up the
ashtray from the table, studied the stylised 'E' that was
the hotel's trademark, and set it down. There was a
suppressed violence about him. It would not have surprised her if the ashtray had shattered in his grip.

Elizabeth took a firm hold on her composure.

'Shouldn't you wait until your wife has seen the place before you decide to rent it?'

He looked up with a gleam in his eyes. 'You are grasping at straws, aren't you, Betsy? Give up. I'm not married. And I have no intention of just going away.'

'Why? It's been years since—whatever it is you think I did to you.'

'I don't take kindly to gold-diggers, Betsy.'

'That's the second time you've used that word. I never asked you for money, Grady. I never asked you for anything you didn't want to give.'

He laughed. 'But you had a way of making me want to give you everything, didn't you? You didn't need to ask.'

She looked him in the eye calmly. 'I feel sorry for you, Grady. It must be hell to think that a woman could only want you because of your father's money.'

'I return the compliment, my dear. It must be hell to know that someday your husband is going to wake up and realise that under that beautiful shell is nothing but greed.' He leaned back and dug a hand into his pocket. 'I hope, for Rick's sake, that he died before he saw through you.'

'Don't talk to me about Rick.' Elizabeth's voice was tightly controlled.

'Why? Do you feel guilty about the way you treated him? Maybe there's hope for you yet.'

Elizabeth let the silence lengthen. Finally she asked, 'How well did you know Rick?'

'Not well. He was my brother's friend, not mine.'

'Well, let me assure you that Rick died happy.'

'I'm delighted to hear it. But I don't think that means that I have to stand by and watch you defraud a friend of my father's. I don't like your little game with Myles, and I don't intend to let you get away with it.'

Elizabeth sipped her coffee and pushed it aside. 'I'm amazed that you're willing to stay anywhere near me,

Grady,' she said coolly. 'If I'm such a witch, what's to prevent me from snaring you again? It would be no real challenge to get you. And it might be rewarding.'

'You couldn't do it. Once bitten, you know—I'm immune to your so-called charms. It wouldn't be the same thing as deceiving two old men.'

'Two? Do you include your father?'

Grady looked a bit chagrinned at his slip. 'Yes, you did make a great impression on my father.'

'And he suggested you rent an apartment in the Englin because he thought I might make a good wife for you?' Elizabeth guessed shrewdly. 'That's positively humorous, Grady. The same man who would have disowned you for marrying me years ago is now trying to matchmake.'

'It's rare for him to be taken in, Betsy. You should consider it a compliment. And believe it or not, I love my father deeply. He's one of the reasons I'm determined to see you back where you belong.'

'And where is that?'

'Scrubbing hall floors in some cheap little motel.'

'I'm glad you've been so straightforward, I appreciate the honesty.' Elizabeth rose. 'Just be sure before you pull the pin out of your little grenade that it isn't going to explode in your hand.'

Elizabeth rubbed a hand wearily across her eyes and tried to concentrate on what Tom Bradford was telling her. 'We'll have to juggle the two conventions,' he said. 'Whoever scheduled them on the same weekend must have been blind.'

'I think it was I who did the scheduling.'

'Oh. Well, you were still blind, Elizabeth. The Midwest cigarette distributors and the Anti-Lung Cancer League in the same hotel? Sharing a floor?' He shook his head. 'We'll have to move the anti-smokers up to the mezzanine floor, because they don't need as much space. But that's going to create a kitchen problem for the banquets.' He nibbled a pencil. 'I think if we. . .'

'Whatever you think best, Tom.'

He looked at her sharply. 'Elizabeth, don't you feel well? I'm sorry I yelled at you. You've looked a little pale all day.'

'Oh, I'm all right. I just didn't get enough sleep last night, that's all.' She had watched the sun rise over Lake Michigan without having slept at all.

'Why don't you go home? There isn't anything here that I can't handle.'

Elizabeth shook her head. 'No, there are a couple of calls coming in.' Her attorney, for one. She had reached Alan's secretary early this morning, but he had been in court, and the girl had promised to have him call back. He hadn't called, and she was getting worried. If Alan told her she couldn't break that lease and get rid of Grady Logan before he destroyed her, she didn't know what she would do. There was a sharp pain in the centre of her back, she realised. The strain was making her physically sick.

Tom was watching her, still plainly concerned. 'Did you have any lunch?'

She thought about it. 'No, I didn't. I forgot.'

'Any breakfast?'

'I wasn't hungry.'

'You're going to be sick if you don't eat, Elizabeth.'

'You're not my father, Tom!' It came out sharper than she had intended. 'I'm sorry. I didn't mean to yell at you. I've . . . there's just something on my mind, that's all.'

'Anything to do with Grady Logan?'

She looked up in surprise. Surely she wasn't that transparent. Tom was just extremely sensitive to her moods, she told herself. 'So you have met him.'

'Oh, yes. Mr Englin called me up to the apartment, after Logan decided to rent it, introduced us, and had me take Logan on up to see the Maxwell. He rented it in about five minutes. A man of definite opinions, I'd say.'

Elizabeth smiled. 'Yes, and most of them as wrong as they are stubborn.' It was the first humour she had seen in the situation all day. 'I'm waiting for Alan to call back; he's trying to find a way to break that lease Myles signed.'

Tom was plainly startled. 'Why? Because Logan's an opinionated so-and-so? Who cares, if he has enough money to pay the rent?'

'Oh, he has plenty of that. You've heard of Whit Logan? The Logan Banks?'

'Hasn't everybody?'

'This is his son. Grady followed his father into finance. There's another son, but I don't know what he does. It isn't banks, though. He has a little more strength of character than Grady does—he decided to make his own way in the world instead of relying on Papa.'

'It seems to me that whatever a son of Whit Logan's did, he'd be building on Papa's name,' Tom interjected mildly.

'You may be right at that.'

'So why do you want to be rid of him? He isn't likely to get in your way.'

'That's what you think, Tom.' Elizabeth toyed with a pencil. 'Plus, it seems, both his father and Myles have concluded that if they can marry us off, it would be a union made in heaven. I'd really just as soon not tell Myles what I really think of Grady Logan.'

'How long have you known him, anyway? I thought Mr Englin said last night he'd never met the man before.'

'He hasn't. But I have—and I'd rather Myles didn't ever know that.'

Tom grinned and sat down on the corner of her desk. 'My God, Saint Elizabeth has a skeleton in her closet after all!'

'I'm no angel, Tom. I've made plenty of mistakes in my day.' She turned towards the window.

Tom slid off the desk and came to stand behind her. He put a gentle hand on her shoulder. 'I'm sorry, Elizabeth. I honestly forgot about your husband.'

'My crowning folly.' Her voice was bitter.

'It isn't your fault the man was a sadist.' He kissed the nape of her neck. His neatly-trimmed beard was scratchy.

Elizabeth stiffened, and Tom sighed and moved away. He reached for a pack of matches on her desk, lit a cigarette, and inhaled deeply. Then, with a troubled look, he tapped the cigarette in the ashtray and said abruptly, 'Elizabeth, why don't you see a doctor? This hang-up of yours. . .'

'I do not need a psychiatrist, Tom.'

'Yes you do. That guy still has you so tied in knots that nobody else can even kiss you. I know he hurt you. . .'

'That's just it, Tom. You don't know. Nobody knows.' Elizabeth turned away from the window just as the intercom on her desk buzzed.

'Mr McConnell's on line three,' the tinny voice of her secretary said.

She picked up the telephone. 'Hi, Alan. What have you found out?' She tapped an eraser on the deskpad.

'Elizabeth, if Myles signed the lease I drew up, you ought to know you can't break it. We wrote it that way, remember? Airtight.'

'I remember. But you can't fault me for trying.'

Alan McConnell laughed. 'There are a couple of ways out.'

'Give them to me quick.'

'If you and the tenant agree you want to break it, you can tear it up together.'

'Not bloody likely.'

'Elizabeth, you shock me.'

'Sorry, Alan. What's the other way?'

'Convince a court that Myles is dangerously imbal-anced.'

Elizabeth laughed in spite of herself. 'Myles? A mental patient?'

'And if you decide to try that, you can find another lawyer to present the case. I don't want to be made a laughing-stock. Tell me, what's so bad about the tenant?'

'I'd rather not go into details, Alan. Especially if I'm stuck with him.'

'I'm afraid you are, until the renewal period comes up. Then you can refuse to renew, and you don't have to give any reasons. But you'd better talk to Myles about it, or he'll renew before you have a chance to say no.'

'By then you can tell the court *I'm* a mental case. Tell Tonya hello for me when you talk to her tonight.'

'Oh, yes. How are my beloved wife and child?'

'Probably going nuts because I left *my* beloved son with them.'

'They'll have a ball. Brian's been pining for Jeremy the whole month he and Tonya have been up there.'

'Are you missing them?'

'You don't really expect me to answer that, do you, Elizabeth? For all I know you have the phone bugged. I'll see you at Vickie's cocktail party on Wednesday and you can tell me all about the weekend.'

'Tonya will miss out on that party, won't she?'

'As she would say—she never misses Vicki's parties. She just tries never to attend them,' Alan said dryly. 'And you can tell me all about this tenant you want to get rid of. It must be a good story or you wouldn't give up the money. I know what those penthouses rent for.'

'There are some things I don't even tell my attorney, Alan.'

'Then you're a fool, darling,' Alan said cheerfully.

Elizabeth cradled the phone and said a word that was, for her, uncharacteristic.

'Your head doorman is supposed to have connections with the Mob. Maybe you can get him to put a contract out on Logan,' Tom suggested lightly.

'Don't joke about Henry's connections with the Mob, Tom.'

'You mean he really has some?'

'Some of his best friends carry guns under their jackets.' Elizabeth shuffled a stack of papers on her desk. 'Will you handle all of the rescheduling on the conventions?'

'Sure. Do you want to manage one of them?'

'I'll take the group you move. They'll probably be the most trouble, and having the general manager babysitting them might soothe the ruffled tempers. That's two weeks from now?'

'Ten days. It's over the weekend—they'll be coming in on Friday. And we don't have many reservations, so perhaps the whole problem will take care of itself.'

'I still can't quite see them sharing the Grand Ballroom. I must have been asleep when I booked that combination.' Elizabeth stared at the folder. 'You'd better hold back a block of rooms, just in case.'

'Is your famous intuition at work again?'

'Call it that if you like. I just have a feeling.'

Tom pushed the notebook back into the leather portfolio on the corner of her desk and stubbed his cigarette out. 'I have tickets to the new comedy at the Arie Crown on Wednesday evening. Would you like to go?'

'Are you sure you can't find a more cheerful companion? Our newest assistant manager has been dying for a little of your attention.'

He shrugged. 'Jill's a nice girl, but I want you.'

'All right, Tom. I'd like to go. Thank you.' The comedy was supposed to be a good one. Perhaps it would be an evening when she wouldn't have to fight her own thoughts.

'But I still wish you'd see a doctor.'

Elizabeth snapped, 'I'll go to the play on the condition you don't refer again to my mental health—or lack of it.'

'I'm sorry, Elizabeth.' The door closed softly behind him.

She sighed. It wasn't right to take out her frustrations on Tom. Just because Grady Logan had reappeared and she was panicky about what she was going to do, was no reason to be sarcastic with Tom.

She walked over to the window. She ought to know better than to go out with Tom; it created too many problems, no matter how much they tried to keep their personal relationship from affecting their work. Tom was an awfully nice guy, though, and sometimes she wondered if she would be happy if she married him. Her common sense told her she wouldn't, but she needed some male companionship. If she chose to let it go no further than companionship, that was her business. And she really had tried to discourage him. She honestly did wish that Tom would start dating Jill, or any of another dozen girls she could name. But he didn't seem to know that the girl was anything more than a new trainee.

'Don't tangle old problems up with new ones,' she told herself. Grady was enough to worry about at any one time. If he told Myles that she'd worked as a chambermaid at a Wisconsin inn that summer that Myles thought she'd been visiting friends. . . Myles' temper was uncertain at best, and the one thing she didn't need was for him to start questioning her story.

It had been years ago, and the whole thing had died down; nobody was concerned any more about who and what Elizabeth Englin was. If Grady dragged the whole mess up again, it would make Myles ill, it would offend Whit so badly he would never want to see anybody named Englin again (which wouldn't be so bad as far as she was concerned, Elizabeth thought, but it would kill Myles), it would drag Jeremy through the mud and probably affect his whole future. No, she couldn't allow that to happen.

But maybe Grady wouldn't tell Myles. To do so would destroy his hold on her, and Elizabeth suspected that Grady would get greater satisfaction out of watching her worry about it than in actually blowing the whistle on her.

There was a tap on her office door. 'Come in, Tom,' she called. She stood at the window, her back to the office, nibbling on a manicured nail. Maybe she'd call Tonya tonight and talk to Jeremy. He'd been away forever. So much for Florence, she thought, and her notions of how the child was too dependent on his mother. He was doing just fine; it was Elizabeth who was homesick.

'What an enchanting picture. Too bad Myles can't see your devotion and worry. Or do you have a special performance for him?'

'Grady!' Elizabeth spun around. 'Who let you in here?'

He shrugged. 'You told me to come in. There was no one in the outer office to announce me, so I just knocked.'

'Well, get out.'

'Are you always so callous to tenants who come bearing money? I came to pay my first quarter's rent. I trust you've discovered by now that you can't break that lease?'

'I've found out that you could.'

'With the consent of both parties, you mean. At least that's what my attorney told me.'

'Of course.' Hating herself for voicing the question, Elizabeth said, 'What is it worth for you to tear up the lease?'

He smiled. 'What are you offering?'

'If you'll tear up the lease and find another apartment . . . I'll pay the rent on it for a year.'

Grady shook his head. 'Mere money? You disappoint me, Betsy. Besides, money doesn't tempt me; you forget that those of us who have always had plenty don't feel the same acquisitiveness about hard cash.'

'Bankers always have an acquisitiveness about hard cash.'

He grinned. 'I have my doubts you have that much tucked away. You're talking a considerable sum; I have expensive tastes. Tell me, do you just draw a salary here or are you a partner?'

'You don't expect me to answer that, do you?'

'No, I guess I don't. Now if you were to stop talking dollars and offer me your lovely self. . .'

She let the silence lengthen as she stared out over the lake. 'What then?'

He spoke softly from just behind her. 'Are you making a proposition, Betsy?'

'No. Just wondering how far you'd go.'

'That's funny. I was wondering the same thing about you.' His hands came to rest on her waist, and he pulled her gently back against him. 'It's just as well you didn't make me an offer, darling—because I hate to have to refuse a lady. I told you last night I'm immune to you —remember?'

He might be immune to her, and his hands were certainly impersonal enough. But she wasn't immune to him. He absently rubbed his chin against her hair, and icicles straightened Elizabeth's spine. She stepped away from him and said, 'If you're determined to keep the Maxwell, then give me the cheque and get out of here.'

His smile told her that she wasn't fooling him. He pulled the slip of paper out of his pocket and waved it under her nose.

She took it and said, 'After this you can pay at the cashier's desk downstairs. They'll give you a receipt.'

'You wouldn't deny me the pleasure of handling the money over in person, would you? The pain of parting with so much cash is deadened by the lovely view.'

'Just go away.'

'Don't you want to hear the conclusions I reached after a long night's thought?

'Not particularly.'

'I was certain you would.' Grady moved a stack of folders on Elizabeth's desk and sat down on the corner of it, folding his arms. She could see the muscles that rippled across his chest and back under the bright-coloured silky shirt he wore. She turned away so that she didn't have to see the strength in his arms.

'I've decided not to tell Myles what I know,' he said.

It was what she had suspected. 'Oh? What's the catch?'

'Not just yet, anyway. I'm going to enjoy watching you squirm.'

'How chivalrous of you.'

'Isn't it? Of course, there's another reason, too.'

'I'm sure you've going to tell me.' Her voice was flippant, but her nerves were screaming. She turned towards the window, fighting for control.

'I might be wrong. After all, you might really have loved Rick.' He studied the back of her blonde head, the flaxen hair pinned into a smooth twist, and the lovely slim fingers tapping nervously on the delicate line of her jaw. 'No comment?'

'What do you expect me to do?' Throw myself at your feet and cry about how much I miss Rick?' Anguish tore at her voice. A wave of black pain washed over her as she remembered the night they had come to tell her Rick was dying. The cab ride to the hospital, the long white halls— all were a blur in her memory. The only thing she remembered clearly was the deep blue of Rick's eyes as he had gripped her hand there in the intensive care unit. He had whispered, 'Take care of Myles, Bet. Tell Jeremy I'm sorry. . .' Her hand had been bruised from his grip for days, long after his funeral was past.

She half consciously flexed her left hand—the one Rick had clung to—and took a deep breath.

Grady raised an eyebrow. 'You do the grieving widow part very well, Betsy. Let me compliment you. One would think it was real.'

'One would be right.'

'Come on, Betsy. He's been dead for years.'

'I've asked you before not to talk to me about Rick. Yes, it's been years—three and a half years—and though I didn't actually see the car crash, I watch it in my nightmares.' Her voice was tortured. It was true. At least once a week she woke up in a cold sweat, seeing the jigsaw puzzle of mangled steel that had been Rick's foreign sports car. Elizabeth took a deep breath. 'Would you please get out of here? I'm going home.'

'Then it would be my pleasure to take you there. I wouldn't want to leave you alone in your upset condition.'

Too late Elizabeth saw the trap she'd sprung on herself. 'That won't be necessary,' she said coolly.

Grady raised an eyebrow. 'How are you going to stop me?'

Elizabeth cleared the top of her desk, picked up her handbag, and silently led the way. In the outer office she stopped to talk to her secretary, hoping that Grady would tire of waiting. But he was perfectly at ease as he stood one step behind her, a head taller despite the high-heeled sandals she wore, watching her sign letters. The secretary was having trouble keeping her eyes off him, and Elizabeth supposed she would have to admit that he was attractive to women. At least, until they got to know him well, she told herself. She decided that tomorrow the secretary would get a lecture for leaving her desk vacant without warning Elizabeth. If that got to be a habit, Grady could make himself at home in her office, and that was just the sort of thing he'd think was fun.

The last letter signed, she had no choice when Grady reached for her arm. 'Ready?'

Silently, she let him guide her out of the office.

'Didn't Myles say the other night that he'd sold the rest of the Englin chain?' he asked, looking around the mezzanine lobby. Her office opened on to a balcony that looked over the lower floor. His eyes rested thoughtfully on the enormous silver and crystal chandelier.

'Yes.'

'I'm surprised you let him do that.'

'It wasn't a question of letting him do anything. The hotels were his. But I agreed with his decision.' She pushed the button for the twenty-third floor.

'When did he sell?'

Elizabeth sighed. Obviously he wasn't going to stop asking questions until he got the answers. The man didn't seem to recognise a brushoff. 'I think you missed your calling when you decided not to be a reporter,' she said resentfully. 'Actually, he didn't sell the hotels. He merged the chain with Hoteliers, Inc., in a partnership deal. They still carry the Englin name, but Hoteliers manages them.'

'That sounds more like you, Betsy. Stockholders benefits must be pretty good. How long ago was this?'

'Three years. After Rick's death and Myles' second heart attack, there was no one to do the necessary travelling.'

'And little Betsy didn't volunteer? You took over the Englin fast enough. Why not all of them?'

'I'm not a tycoon. And I managed the Englin before Rick died.'

'Making yourself indispensible? Wise move. I'm surprised you didn't encourage Myles to sell this one too. It must tie you down to hold this job. But then, I can't make up my mind as to whether you're the power-hungry managing type or the kind who just wants to sit in the sun on a Caribbean island for the rest of her life and have the dividend cheques direct-deposited.'

'I knew I shouldn't have let him sell the one in the

Bahamas,' Elizabeth said thoughtfully. 'It had its own beach.'

'I can't imagine why you want to hang on to this hotel.' There was puzzlement in his tone.

'Because I want it for. . .' She stopped dead. For Jeremy, of course, but why tell Grady that? She'd have that problem to face soon enough.'

'For what? Or for whom?' Grady asked.

The elevator whooshed to a halt.

'Got a new boy-friend who's always wanted to own a hotel?' he speculated.

'Would it be any of your business if I did?'

'I don't imagine Myles would like it.'

'You'd be surprised. Myles seldom disapproves of anything I do.' Elizabeth reached for her key. 'Good afternoon, Grady.'

'I'll bet you even charmed the doctor out of spanking you when you were born,' he said admiringly and followed her out of the elevator. 'I'm invited in to have tea with your grandfather.' He seemed to delight in giving the term a sarcastic twist.

'Your invitation or his?' Elizabeth asked tartly.

'Now, Betsy, that's unworthy of you. Mine, of course. Haven't you learned yet that I generally get what I want?'

'A lesson learned at your father's knee, no doubt.'

'It could make for some interesting fireworks, since both of us are used to manipulating everyone around us.'

Elizabeth didn't answer.

Myles was waiting for them at the door, and Florence was just wheeling the tea cart down the hall.

'You're just in time,' Myles said. 'I was about to start without you. I didn't think anything Grady did could get you out of the office early, Elizabeth.'

Elizabeth didn't bother to reply. 'I'm going to change my clothes, Myles. I'll be back later.' Much later, she added to herself. Three hours later should do it.

'You have ten minutes, and then I'm coming after you,' Grady said softly. 'I don't like my tea cold.'

'So pour it yourself.' She flung the words over her shoulder as she started down the hall.

CHAPTER THREE

HER bedroom was invitingly cool and dim, the shades drawn to shut out the glaring sun. Elizabeth threw her handbag across the room and flung herself down on the ruffled organdie spread. The pillowslip was cool against her flushed cheek, and in the quiet her tense body gradually began to relax. It wasn't fair that her ordered life was being ripped to shreds. She'd been caught in the cycle of grief over Rick's death far longer than normal. He'd been a mainstay for her, helping her to adjust to the idea of bringing up Jeremy. Elizabeth, far from maternal on the best of days, had had difficulty in accepting motherhood.

Then Rick had died in that grinding hell of ripped steel, and she'd been shattered. In the three years since the accident she'd put her life painfully back together, and now Grady was insisting on pouring salt into her yet-unhealed wounds.

She let her eyes close, longing for the release sleep would bring. She was exhausted, physically and emotionally worn. The weekend had been difficult. Tonya was her closest friend, but Elizabeth hadn't been able to share even with her what was uppermost in her mind. Tonya didn't know about that summer she'd spent in Bridgedale; no one did. It had bothered her much more than she'd expected to go back. Even the inn itself being gone hadn't eased the pain. Several times she'd seen Tonya looking at her with a question in her eyes. But Elizabeth had passed it off, or changed the subject, and Tonya was too good a friend to probe.

Elizabeth sighed and pushed herself up from the bed. Much as she longed to lie here the rest of the day, she knew it would upset Myles and convince Grady that she was an even better actress than he'd expected.

She pulled the pins out of her hair, brushed it out, and drew it back with a big clasp at the nape of her neck. She exchanged the elegant raw silk suit for coffee-coloured slacks and a yellow pullover with a tiny design in the same coffee colour. She patted cold water on her eyelids, repaired her make-up and went back to the living room.

As she came in, Grady—to all appearances absorbed in his conversation with Myles—glanced at his watch and smiled. Elizabeth unwillingly looked at the porcelain-faced mantel clock and could have kicked herself in aggravation. She had met his deadline. She wondered if he would have come and got her if she hadn't shown up. Probably he would have. He had meant what he said about getting what he wanted. It was a habit of his. And the brute was big enough that he could have carried out his threat. Not that he would have been physical about it, she told herself. Grady had plenty of experience in persuasion.

She poured her tea into an eggshell china cup, added lemon, and curled up in a chair near the fireplace. It was too warm for a fire, but the firebox was full of green plants and cut flowers. Florence was a wizard with flowers, Elizabeth thought absently as she sipped her tea. She really should observe the woman more closely. She herself couldn't put a rose in a vase and make it look attractive.

Tomorrow she'd go up to the penthouse floor and walk through the Carlisle. It was the next apartment to be completely refurbished. How long had it been since she'd been in there? Elizabeth tried to remember. Had it been when that movie producer had rented it while he was on location? He'd had some marvellous parties up there. Marvellous if you weren't the one who had to repair the damage, she muttered to herself.

'Isn't that so, Elizabeth?' Myles asked.

Unwilling to admit that their conversation had been passing her by. Elizabeth nodded her head vaguely. 'Of course, Myles,' she said.

Instantly she knew she should have been paying attention, for Grady looked at her with a warm, intimate smile and said, 'Splendid. I'll be looking forward to it.' He set his teacup down and added, 'Myles, I really must go. I have a lot of arrangements to make before the weekend. Elizabeth, I'll see you on Wednesday, then. I'll find my own way out.'

After he had gone, Elizabeth sat motionless, her cup and saucer frozen in her hands. 'Myles?' she finally said.

'Yes, dear?' He reached for a small table and pulled it over to his chair.

'What did I just agree to do?'

Myles looked up from the hand of Vegas solitaire he was dealing. 'Aren't you feeling well?'

'I'm feeling fine.'

'You look a little pale today. And you were flushed when you came in. Do you think you should see a doctor?'

'Myles! Just tell me what I said I'd do!'

'Grady asked you to come to a dinner party he's giving Saturday. I said I thought you'd be delighted, and you said. . .'

'I know what I said! Oh, damn.'

'What's the matter? Do you have other plans?'

'No. I mean, yes! I'm not going to. . .' She swallowed her protest when she saw the quizzical look on his face. 'So what's the nonsense about seeing me Wednesday?'

Myles turned over a card, considered it carefully, and played it. 'You also said you'd get him an invitation to Vicki Andrews' cocktail party on Wednesday, and go with him.'

Elizabeth put her head down into her hands. Never again would she let her mind wander when that man was anywhere close, she vowed bitterly.

'You are going, aren't you?' Myles asked.

'I suppose so. I hadn't given it much thought.'

'You should. You know Vicki Andrews is president of the Chicago League. It would be worthwhile to keep the lines of communication open, especially if you want her to recommend that the league have its débutante ball at the Englin again this year.' Another card went on to the pile.

'You're right, of course. And I was planning to go. Only. . .' She groped for an excuse. 'Only I'm going to the theatre with Tom that night.'

'The party will be over in plenty of time. And I wish you'd stop dating Tom, anyway, Elizabeth. He's a nice boy, but it's just not a good idea to socialise with your employees. Anyway, this just gives you another reason to go. Dear, most of the people Grady will meet there, outside of the ones in the financial community, will be strangers to him. You know most of them. Give the boy a hand. You can get an invitation for him, can't you?'

'Of course. But I'd have thought he'd be adept at making new friends all by himself by now. He's thirty years old!' Elizabeth's tone was dry.

Myles looked at her with an odd expression and Elizabeth warned herself to be more careful. He was surprised that she knew Grady's age, that was obvious. She had, so far as Myles knew, just met Grady yesterday. It wasn't like her to be so quick with a negative judgment.

But he simply said, 'It wouldn't be a bad idea for you to cultivate the friendship, Elizabeth. I wouldn't be surprised if Whit turns the whole show over to Grady one of these days. It's obviously what he's being groomed for. And you never know when you'll need a loan.'

'There are other bankers. And I wouldn't bet on Whit Logan turning anything over to anybody. That man will die in a boardroom.'

Myles made no comment. He turned his attention back

to the deck of cards. 'I don't know why you've taken such an instant dislike to Grady, my dear, but do this for his father's sake if not for his.'

Elizabeth choked on a slightly hysterical laugh. The idea that she would go out of her way to please Whit Logan! Well, the sooner she got herself out of this, the better. She stood up.

'Where are you going, Elizabeth?'

'To cultivate a friendship,' she tossed over her shoulder.

'I'm glad you're going to be sensible about it.'

She had to threaten the desk clerk to get Grady's telephone number. Elizabeth had made the policy herself; all tenants were required to give their unlisted numbers to the desk, but the hotel solemnly promised never to divulge the information or use it except in emergencies. Now it took a direct order from the general manager to get the number, and when she dialled, the telephone buzzed softly in her ear. She had almost given up when it clicked and a deep voice said, 'Logan.'

'Grady. . .'

'Betsy, darling, I wondered how long it would take you to come up with an excuse. You disappoint me; it's been almost twenty minutes.'

Elizabeth snapped, 'It took me ten to get your number.'

He just laughed. 'Considering the telephone was just installed today and it's unlisted, I congratulate you. Actually, I hoped you wouldn't get it. That way you couldn't back out.'

'I could stand you up.'

'But you wouldn't.'

'Why not? Don't give me too much credit for being a lady, unless you're prepared to extend it all the time. Since I'm going to the cocktail party anyway, and since I don't want to explain to Myles why I'm not going with you, you can pick me up at six o'clock.'

'You amaze me. I was certain you were going to tell me

you couldn't get an invitation for me. Which I wouldn't have believed.'

'Assuming, of course, that I can get you an invitation. There's no sense in quibbling about that. But I'm going to be terribly busy this weekend. I have a fund-raising ball to go to Saturday evening, and I just can't make it for dinner.'

'Somehow that doesn't surprise me.' His tone was matter-of-fact.

'I appreciate the honour and all . . .'

'I know. But you have to have dinner somewhere. We don't care if you eat and run. I think some of my guests will be going to the dance anyway—if it's the Chicago League thing you're talking about?'

'I'm not coming to dinner, Grady.'

'Just a few people—six or eight. All you have to do is look beautiful, and since you've had twenty-five years of practice at doing that. . .'

'I am not coming!'

There was a moment of silence. Then Grady asked, a regretful tone in his voice, 'Is that your final word?'

'No. This one is—goodbye!'

'Then would you be an angel and tell Myles I'll be down to talk to him after dinner? I have a fascinating story to tell him. It would go well with his brandy and cigar.'

'You wouldn't do it.'

'You know, I rather think I would. After all, it's only a nice neighbourly gesture to come to my party. It wouldn't hurt you to be friendly. Besides, how do you ever expect to convince Myles you can't stand me if you won't even give me a fair chance? To say nothing of what sort of trouble I'll have convincing my father that my charm just isn't working on you.'

'Tell him you sent it out for repairs. If I give in on this, where is this blackmail going to stop?'

'That's such a nasty word, Betsy. Remember, I'm taking a risk, too.'

'Oh, really? What?'

'You could go to that cocktail party, introduce me around, and then whisper behind my back that I was really not the thing at all and that no one should have anything to do with me.'

'You're right, I could.' Elizabeth's voice was rapt.

'And you could come to my dinner decked out like a prostitute or something. . .'

'Or a former hotel maid?'

'My thought exactly.'

'I'd disgrace you.'

'That's what has me worried.'

'You don't sound worried. And if you're so concerned, why not avoid the whole problem by letting me stay at home?'

'As far as the cocktail party is concerned, I'd rather have you on my arm where I can hear what you're saying. And for the dinner, you do have a good reputation in this town—undeserved as it might be.'

'Thanks. Why do I not feel complimented?'

'So I'd like to propose a little deal. You come to the cocktail party and my dinner, act like the perfect lady you've practised so hard to be, and get me off to a good start with the society figures, and I won't tell Myles about Betsy Ames' antics up in Bridgedale.'

'Do you mean it?'

'I mean it. It's no big deal to me, after all. I've been thinking about it, and I've ended up almost admiring you for getting away with it. I'm glad it wasn't me you nailed with that little game, of course, but as long as it wasn't, what difference does it make to me?'

'Do I have your promise never to tell Myles?'

'On my honour.'

'Grady, you have no honour.'

'You have just as much reason to trust me as I do to trust you.' There was an instant of silence. 'Are you coming?'

Elizabeth told herself that there was a catch somewhere. But the important thing right now was that Myles did not know anything about Bridgedale, for if Grady let drop that they'd met before Elizabeth didn't want to think about the consequences. If Myles found out that she'd lied to him about that summer. . . 'I'll come.'

'Good. See you at six, day after tomorrow, for the cocktail party.'

'If I can get you an invitation,' Elizabeth said sourly.

'How could you fail?' And Grady cradled the phone.

Elizabeth sat there with the receiver in her hand for a moment longer, thinking, 'I've been conned. I know I've been conned.' But in the back of her mind was unexplainable trust in Grady. He'd never broken a promise, she remembered, and told herself sharply, 'That's because he never made any.' In any case, she was committed, and she put the phone down with the distinct feeling that she'd been the loser in that round.

'I do so love Mother's cocktail parties, don't you, Elizabeth? And where did you find that handsome man?'

Elizabeth answered without losing a beat. 'I ordered him from the Penney's catalogue.' She turned to face the dark-haired girl in a flame-orange dress who had asked the questions. 'Hi, Anne.'

'Hi. I wonder if they make one my size,' Vicki Andrews' daughter Anne murmured. Her dark-brown eyes, expertly enlarged with bronze shadow, rested thoughtfully on Grady, who was leaning on the bar across the room.

Elizabeth looked down at the girl with a trace of impatience in her eyes. Anne was nineteen, and the best word anyone could find for her was Tonya's—she called Anne a vamp. 'I know it's old-fashioned,' Tonya had said the night, almost a year before, when Anne had had her début at the Chicago League's ball, 'but the girl is a vamp and that's the only word that fits.'

Elizabeth wasted a moment wishing that Tonya was here instead of in Wisconsin; she wouldn't have hesitated to put Anne in her place, no matter who the girl's mother was. Elizabeth knew better than to say anything herself. Vicki was fiercely defensive of her spoiled, beautiful daughter.

'No doubt he's just your size,' Elizabeth murmured. 'And I was thinking of sending him back anyway. He just isn't quite what the catalogue promised.'

Anne was again watching Grady. 'I did see you come in with him, didn't I? What's his name?'

'Grady Logan.'

Anne's eyes widened. 'As in the Logan Banks?' She turned to look more closely at Elizabeth.

'Got it in one.' Elizabeth privately added her congratulations. Anne was on her toes, that was sure. She'd inherited a great deal of Vicki's aggressive intelligence.

'And he's handsome, too. God, some men have all the luck.' Anne meditatively sipped her drink. 'And you really don't want him?'

'Would it make any difference to you if I did?' Elizabeth knew her claws were showing, but the words were out before she could stop them.

'I know they call you the Ice Maiden, but I didn't know why,' Anne said. 'Do you mean you're just throwing him away?' She turned away, not waiting for an answer.

Alan McConnell put an arm around Elizabeth. 'Since Tonya's out of town, I can flirt, right?' he asked.

Elizabeth laughed. 'Right.' She turned her cheek for his light kiss. 'How is Tonya?'

'She can't wait to get home. She told me last night that if she had to go another week without seeing Lord and Taylor she'd come home in a cardboard box.'

'I hope Jeremy isn't driving her nuts.'

'Oh, no. He's keeping Brian occupied, and they're both out of her hair that way. Who's the dark-haired doll you were just talking to?'

'Male or female?'

'The female of the species, darling. I generally don't lust after the males.' He drained his glass and set it aside. 'Though you might as well not bother. She just went after your other dark-haired doll—the one Tonya would have been asking you about. That's Whit Logan's son, isn't it?'

Elizabeth didn't bother to answer. She looked over her shoulder just in time to see Anne turn ever so casually into Grady's path as he started across the room with their drinks. For a brief instant, she was almost in his arms. Then she smiled meltingly up at him, fluttered the lashes around the absurdly big brown eyes, and said a few words. Grady laughed and came on across the room.

'I wish girls would do that for me,' Alan grumbled.

'They would, dear, if Tonya didn't have such fearfully long fingernails.' Then, thoughtfully, 'I really should congratulate Baby Anne. That was a coup—and very nicely carried out. I wouldn't have had enough guts at nineteen.'

'Is that all the age she is? Who is she, anyway?'

'She's Vicki's daughter, Anne. If she seriously goes after Grady, it would be a relationship made on the New York Stock Exchange. Come to think of it, with all the banks their families own, the banns might have to be approved by the federal government so they don't get involved in anti-trust action.' It was said under her breath; then she smiled at Grady and reached for the wineglass he held out.

But Alan had heard, and there was a laugh in his voice as he introduced himself to Grady. Elizabeth sipped her wine and let her eyes wander over the room. Anne had returned to a group near the terrace doors and was paying not a bit of attention to Grady. Elizabeth reluctantly gave the girl credit; she knew her business and had obviously recognised him as a man who liked to do his own pursuing. So Anne was going to let him pursue.

Alan chatted for a few moments and then excused himself. Grady reached for Elizabeth's hand. 'How's the wine?' he asked.

'It's good. There's Vicki, by the fireplace. Shall we go over while she's free?'

'Unless you'd rather find some place to be alone so we can neck.' Then, delighted, he said, 'Betsy, darling, I didn't dream you still knew how to blush!'

'Only because the suggestion is repulsive.'

'Shall we find somewhere private so you can prove that?' he murmured. 'You never used to think I was repulsive. For now, though, I just can't give up the opportunity to meet this paragon of society, Mrs Andrews.' His hand resting lightly at the back of her dress sent shivers up her spine. 'Don't tell anybody,' Grady added in a conspiratorial whisper, 'but actually I think cocktail parties are the invention of the devil.'

'I know.' Elizabeth spoke in a casual tone, determined to get the conversation back to neutral ground. 'Everybody drifting around with an axe to grind, and at the end of the party no one can remember whether they succeeded.'

'And in the meantime they're wasting perfectly good Scotch. What's your axe?'

'The Chicago League is deciding on a place to hold its débutante ball. What's yours?'

'Isn't it obvious? Andrews is one of my colleagues.'

'Is that all? I expected something exciting. It's incredible how many bankers there are in this town.'

'Is that a slur on the profession?'

'Only if you want to take it that way. One thing you do have to say about Vicki's parties, though—you meet everyone who is anyone at them, between his connections and hers.'

Grady looked with disfavour around the room. 'If you say so.'

'I imagine after New York City it looks a little tame.'

'I wouldn't know. I haven't spent much time there the last few years.'

'Oh? I assumed you'd been under your father's wing all this time.'

'No. I just rejoined the corporation a year ago.'

Elizabeth wanted to pursue the subject, but she couldn't find the right words. If Grady hadn't been in the banking business with his father, what had he been doing? And why?

Vicki Andrews looked up from the woman she was talking to and smiled brilliantly at Elizabeth. She was a well-preserved forty-five and—as Tonya said—knew it. 'Liz! I saw you come in, but I couldn't break away. We must get together soon; I need to talk to you about arrangements for the débutante ball.'

'Why don't you come and lunch with me one day next week? Shall we say Tuesday?' Elizabeth hoped the triumph she felt didn't show in her voice.

'Wednesday would be better. I'll call you the first of the week. I'll ask Tonya McConnell to join us, since she's vice-president this year. She will be back in town by then, won't she?'

Elizabeth assented, thinking how typical it was of Vicki that whatever date was suggested would be inconvenient. But she wanted the ball to be held at the Englin, and for that she could put up with nearly any amount of aggravation from Vicki Andrews. She was just glad that Vicki was already making arrangements. The ball wasn't for a few months yet, but that time would slip by quickly.

'And who is this you have with you, Liz?' Vicki asked, batting her eyelashes just a bit at Grady.

Elizabeth introduced him, and Vicki's eyelashes speeded up. 'Josh mentioned you just the other day, Grady. How young you are for such a position of authority. I'm sure we'll be seeing a great deal of you.' She signalled her husband. 'Would you join us tomorrow— just a small party, for dinner?'

'I'd enjoy that, Mrs Andrews.' His eyes, mocking, met Elizabeth's.

She raised an eyebrow. It seemed Grady didn't need her help after all. Or maybe Vickie had seen Anne's manoeuvre and had decided to give the romance a push.

Vicki was going on, 'And you must find time for the Chicago League's dance on Saturday night. It's just a small thing—a fund-raiser for handicapped children. And it's right at the Englin. Wouldn't he love it, Liz?'

'I'm sure he would, Vicki.'

Grady said he'd think about it and moved a step away to talk to Josh Andrews.

'Nice-looking man. How'd you manage to get him on the string so quickly?' Vicki asked dryly.

'His father and Myles are close friends.'

Vicki's eyes returned from assessing Grady to rest on Elizabeth. 'Well, do give the rest of Chicago a chance at him, Liz.

'He's a free agent.' Anne has no competition to worry about from me, she added to herself.

'How's Jeremy?'

'Fine, thank you. He's gone to Wisconsin to stay with Tonya for a week.'

'Your devotion to him is so charming I'm surprised you've let him go,' Vicki said gently.

An elderly woman fluttered up and took Vicki's arm. 'Darling, you must tell me all about the McConnells,' she whispered.

What new gossip was going the rounds about Tonya

and Alan? Elizabeth wondered. Probably just the fact that Alan was here alone. She found Grady's hand on her elbow. As he guided her through the crowded room, he said, 'You must want that débutante ball badly to put up with her.'

Elizabeth laughed. 'I didn't see you turning down that dinner invitation.'

'And you don't mind if she calls you Liz?'

'Of course I mind. I just don't tell her.'

'How noble of you! Now that we've both ground our axes, shall we go?'

'It can't be too soon for me.' Elizabeth set her half-filled glass down on the nearest table. 'I think I've had too much wine, anyway.'

'Shall we have dinner?' Grady pulled up the sleeve of his pale blue suit and checked his watch. 'It's early yet; surely someone can fit us in without a reservation.'

'No, thanks. The deal included the cocktail party, not dinner. I trust I've lived up to your expectations?'

'Oh, yes. I've met more high society dames here today than I could in my normal way of life in a month. I never realised what a power you must be in this city. How you got there I'll never know. But then Chicago's a brash town—it always has been.'

'I know. Mrs Astor I'm not.'

'No. And not a Cabot or a Lodge, either. How fortunate for you that Rick wasn't from Boston; you wouldn't even have been in the running. But then, if he had been, you wouldn't have met him.' He held the street door for her. 'How did you meet Rick, by the way?'

Elizabeth said composedly. 'It's all hidden in the foggy reaches of my distant past. And I can't think you'd find it exciting anyway. Perhaps I should warn you that that little brunette dish who almost ran into you is Vicki's daughter.'

He whistled softly. 'Why warn me? Is there something

more here that I should know? Or don't you think I can watch out for myself?'

'Maybe it's Anne who I should warn,' Elizabeth said acidly.

Grady laughed and hailed a cruising taxi. 'Your concern is welcome but misplaced, Betsy. After all, any man who has survived you can laugh at all of the amateurs.'

Elizabeth bit her tongue and didn't answer.

'How lucky can I be?' he mused. 'I've never got a cab this fast. I thought you were crazy when you insisted on getting a cab to come out here, you know. Isn't that a Porsche I saw eating its head off in the parking space reserved for the general manager?'

'Yes.'

He helped her into the cab. 'Your mode of transportation has changed since Bridgedale. Then you were riding city buses.' He told the driver, 'The Englin, please.'

'Your memory is at fault. Bridgedale had no city buses. I walked. I never use the Porsche in town; it's too much of a pain to park it. I thought that would have been obvious to you.'

'I'd forgotten the inconveniences of big cities; I had just been longing for their advantages.'

Elizabeth's curiosity became unbearable. 'Just where have you been for the last few years? Hiding from the law in Podunk Center?'

'Denver.'

'Hardly a small town.'

'No. But at least you can still park a car on Colfax Avenue. Sometimes you can even park within six blocks of where you're going.' He put an arm across the back of the seat. Elizabeth moved away. 'Tell me, in all these long years, didn't you ever get curious about where I was?'

Elizabeth shrugged. 'No. Why should I? I just assumed you had run to Daddy when he snapped his fingers.'

'I didn't.'

'Spare me the details. There's a certain amount of evidence that can't be ignored. I hardly think Whit would have made you a vice-president if he didn't approve of what you were doing.'

He let the subject drop. 'Who's Alan McConnell, by the way?'

'My attorney.'

'Oh? How do you pay your bills? I saw him kiss you.'

'You couldn't have. Your back was turned.'

'I have antennae that pick up that sort of thing.'

'Well, they were out of order today. Alan's wife is my dearest friend.'

'I don't imagine that would stop you if he was worth enough.'

'One kiss at a cocktail party does not mean I'm having an affair with the man.'

'That's true. If you were having an affair, you would be bright enough to keep it a secret. It's a matter of experience, I'm sure. Are you certain you don't want to have dinner with me?'

'Never more so in my life. Besides, I have a date.'

'Such a pity. I was looking forward to an introduction to the best dining spot in this city, with a lovely lady by my side.'

'Grady, the cabby doesn't care. You can stop impressing everybody now.'

'I wasn't flattering you. Tell me, would Jeremy object if you had dinner with me?'

So he had overheard Vicki. 'Probably,' Elizabeth smiled. Her small son had, on occasion, thrown a fit when she went out for an evening, especially if he didn't care for her date.

'Is he your newest love? What is his money in?'

Elizabeth debated saying, 'Baseball cards and candy bars,' but she thought better of it.

'Or doesn't he have any? Is he your one true love, the one you want the Englin for?'

'I don't understand why you think it's any of your business. We made a deal, didn't we?'

'Oh, yes. But that doesn't mean I forget all about your little affairs—just that I don't tell Myles.'

'You're a true gentleman,' Elizabeth said, her voice heavy with sarcasm.

'That's the difference between you and me. I never said I was anything I'm not,' Grady pointed out as the cab screeched to a halt in front of the Englin. 'Was Vicki right in her suspicions, by the way?'

'Which ones? She has plenty.' Elizabeth's voice was dry. She slid out of the cab, her jade-green cocktail dress revealing a shapely leg.

'Nice legs.' Grady handed the cabby a bill and reached for Elizabeth's arm. 'But then they always were.' She neatly avoided his hand. 'Vicki said something about being surprised you'd let your Jeremy go away. Are you worried about him?'

'Of course,' Elizabeth said, raising her eyebrows as if surprised that he had asked. 'He's by far the most charming male I've ever met. I simply couldn't live without him.'

She smiled at Henry, who touched his cap as he pushed the revolving door for her. The look Grady got from the doorman, she couldn't help noticing, was much less respectful. The grapevine was apparently working overtime.

They were waiting for an elevator by the time Grady replied. 'And you think you love him?'

'I know I do.' She stepped into the car and held the door open till he'd recovered his balance. 'Does that surprise you?' she asked kindly.

'No, it doesn't. Love—Betsy Ames' speciality, given away liberally and without prejudice to anyone who has sufficient cash to deserve it. What's Jeremy's money in, anyway?'

'His interests are diversified.' Elizabeth watched the floor numbers light and blink out as the elevator rose.

'I suppose that means he's a multi-millionaire. Well, with the kind of seed money you have at hand now, I suppose we couldn't expect you to stick to younger sons like me or heir apparents like Rick. It must have been a blow to you to find yourself free of your husband but with Myles still around your neck.'

'Have you had your blood pressure checked lately, Grady?' Elizabeth asked sweetly.

He ignored the question. 'And in the meantime, Jeremy's up in Wisconsin and you're playing around down here. Aren't you worried? What if he's up there having an affair with another woman? Tonya—isn't that the name you used?'

'Oh, that's impossible. Besides, Tonya is Alan's wife— remember? The one who's my dearest friend?'

'How cozy to keep it all in the family. You're damned sure of yourself, Betsy. Or you have a lot of confidence in him.'

'No, I simply know him too well. Jeremy has never confined his affections to one woman at a time. There have always been at least five in his life; I think the present count is up around twenty.'

'But you're sure you'll be the winner?'

Cool green eyes flicked over him without interest, and Elizabeth shrugged. 'He wants the Englin, you see.'

'Badly enough to pay for it with a wedding ring?'

'Perhaps. Who cares? If I don't mind, why should you?'

And then she knew she'd gone too far. Grady seized her arms and dragged her roughly against him. 'I wouldn't mind, if he was another fortune-hunter like yourself. It would be damned funny to see him take the Englin away from you and then kick you out on the street. But he's just another poor stiff who's been dumb enough to look into those witch's eyes of yours and fall under your spell. And someday he'll wake up to find himself a couple of million dollars poorer, and you'll be gone, and you won't even have cared enough about the poor sucker to shed a phoney tear while you stab him in the back.'

'You're hurting me.' Elizabeth tried to twist away, but Grady's grip on her arms tightened.

'It's nothing compared to what I plan to do to you,' he said viciously. 'If I'm the only one around who has survived your assault undamaged, then I consider it my duty to pay you back for your little tricks. You aren't going to have it all your own way, any more.'

Somehow he had backed her into a corner so she couldn't move, and his hands cupped her face, thumbs resting on her temples.

Her throat was so tight that she couldn't even whimper. Was he really so angry that he would do her actual harm? She had been concerned for days about what he might tell Myles, but for the first time she was actually afraid of him.

'I could crack your lovely little skull,' he said softly.

She seized the last of her poise, and said, 'Clark Gable played that scene much better. If you don't mind, we've arrived.' Her knees were shaking as she pushed past him to the open door.

CHAPTER FOUR

'I REALLY wish you'd have a steak,' Tom said.

Elizabeth gave him a long, level look and repeated her order of an omelette to the waiter. 'If I were to eat a steak at this hour, I'd never get to sleep,' she told Tom.

'It obviously wouldn't be anything new. You look as if you haven't been to bed in a week.'

'Thanks,' Elizabeth muttered under her breath as he gave his order. She sipped her wine and said, 'Now, if you don't mind, please stop acting like my keeper and tell me what you thought of the play.'

'If you want me to stop being your keeper, then you stop acting as if you need one. With Jeremy out of town it's your perfect opportunity to get rested up. And instead, you're so nervy that whenever anyone says your name you jump a foot.' He lit a cigarette and flipped the spent match into an ashtray with a flick of his wrist.

'The play, Tom. What did you think of the play?'

Tom sighed. 'Obviously you don't want to talk about whatever it is that's bothering you.'

'And I'd rather not think about it, either.'

He reached across the table. 'Let's start all over, all right? We came in here, sat down, you ordered an omelette, and I said, "That sounds good, Elizabeth!"'

She smiled in spite of herself. 'They do make incredible omelettes here. I think it's the spices—I'll have to ask Florence.' She sipped her wine. 'And speaking of Jeremy being out of town—I got a postcard from him today.'

'What's going on?'

'I don't know—it just had his name on it.' At Tom's expression, Elizabeth giggled. 'There isn't much room on a postcard, you know, and Jeremy's handwriting isn't very precise yet. It had a picture of a museum in Milwaukee on it, though, so I assume Tonya's giving him a dose of culture.'

'Or else Jeremy thought it was a pretty building.'

'Possibly. I hadn't thought of that. Maybe he'll be an architect.'

'Would that bother you?'

'If he didn't want to run the hotel? No, I don't think it would. I'd like to see him in the business, but honestly, Tom, when Jeremy's out of college I'll still have twenty years before I'm ready to retire. I'm not the type to sit in a chair and knit, and I never have gone in for volunteer work. I don't know what I'd do with myself if I had to abdicate.'

'Take a trip around the world.'

She considered it. 'No, there's no purpose in it. You see, I'm just too efficient to enjoy anything like that. I'd consider it a waste of time, unless somebody would commission me to do a guidebook, or something, and I hardly think my talents lie in that direction.'

Tom leaned back in his chair to let the waiter place his beef Stroganoff in front of him.

Elizabeth cut into her omelette and watched mushrooms ooze on to the plate.

'You could always get married again and have a family.'

'You're getting on to dangerous ground again, Tom,' she warned.

'Don't you want more children?'

'Why? One can give you as many grey hairs as a dozen can. Especially the way Jeremy is—always sick or hurt.' She put down her fork. 'Tom, you have this lovely ideal of what a woman should be—ruffles and chocolate-chip cookies and handmade snowflakes on the Christmas tree.

I'm not like that. I'm tailored suits and chateaubriand and balance sheets. I can never be the perfect woman. In fact, I'm probably the world's lousiest mother. I let the kid stay up too late, and I swear in front of him, and I push him aside whenever something more important comes up.'

'That's not true, Elizabeth.'

'It's true enough that I feel guilty about it.'

'If you're such a lousy mother, why did you have Jeremy?'

'Because I didn't know I was going to be a lousy mother, and by the time I found out, I'd already lost his guarantee card.'

Tom grinned. 'Why have you been going around in such a blue funk all week, then, if it isn't that you miss him?'

'I never said I didn't miss him,' Elizabeth corrected. 'If anything happened to him, I'd be ten times worse than I was when Rick died. But really, can you see me as a grandmother?'

'You won't exactly fit the stereotype.'

'I'm glad you see my point.' She pushed the rest of the omelette aside.

Tom started to say something about it, but when she glared at him, he shut up, stared at his plate, and didn't say anything for a full minute. Then he looked up and said, 'Did your secretary catch up with you this afternoon?'

'What about? I was in the office until almost five.'

'That magazine reporter called. He's running behind schedule and wants to change his appointment to next week, instead of tomorrow.'

'Well, that's a blessing. I'd forgotten all about it. Why did Myles have to do this to me right now?'

'Do you really want me to repeat it? You already have it memorised.'

Elizabeth glared at him. 'And you just sit there and grin. Why don't you talk to the reporter?'

'You're the one with a balance sheet for a brain; you just told me all about it. Besides, my name isn't Englin, and I wouldn't look nearly as nice as you do draped against the grand staircase in an evening gown.'

'Is there going to be a photographer, too?'

'I assume so. And don't blame Mr Englin for this. He merely agreed that it would be good publicity for the hotel. The idea originated at the head of your stag line—remember?'

'Corbin Evans may run the hotels Myles used to own, but he isn't at the head of my stag line. Where do you pick up these nineteen-forties' phrases, Thomas?'

'Try telling Corbin that he isn't your favourite.'

'I have. He isn't getting any farther with me than you are.'

'I know, Elizabeth; that's the only thing that keeps me from wiping the floor with that handsome face every time he walks in the front door. He's about due for another visit, isn't he?'

'Who keeps track?' Elizabeth shrugged. She hated to admit it to Tom, but she was hoping that Corbin wouldn't be back in town for a while. The last few times he had been in Chicago he had pressured her to have an affair with him. They had always had such fun that it had taken her by surprise when he'd suddenly wanted to get serious. Though, of course, serious was hardly the word. All Corbin wanted was a playmate. His wife had divorced him when she discovered that his job was more important than she was; Corbin had made it quite plain that he would never marry again.

'Sounds as if you aren't looking forward to his next visit, either,' Tom guessed.

'He is beginning to sound like a broken record,' she

admitted. 'It would be a lot more sensible for you to stop scrapping over me and take our new assistant manager out. Something even tells me she's the domestic type.'

'It wouldn't be the homemade cookies she's been bringing to the office, would it?' Tom asked dryly. 'She's a nice kid, but I just don't find her irresistible.'

'Give her a chance. She might just need some practice.'

'Are you promoting fraternisation among the employees?'

'Not exactly, but neither do I think Jill should be off-limits just because she works for the Englin. How is she doing, by the way?'

'Really well. She's got another ten days of orientation and training, and she'll be ready to take over her regular shifts. Her past experience really tells, even if it was only a small hotel she worked for. I think we should make a stronger point of experience when we hire, Elizabeth.'

'We will, Tom. And I think you've done a good job of training her, too. Now if you'd just stand back and take a good look at her as a woman. . .'

'You really know how to deflate a guy's ego. I'm so important to you that you're trying to give me away.'

Elizabeth smiled. 'Comfort yourself with the thought that I do the same with Corbin.'

'I know. Why don't you just dump him entirely? The only thing Corbin wants is a community-property share of all that Hoteliers stock you own.'

'Corbin wouldn't appreciate your saying that. And it isn't true.'

'You're fooling yourself, then, Elizabeth. Do you really think he's in love with you?'

'I'm not that foolish, Tom. But Corbin wouldn't marry me—or any woman—even if she owned every share of Hoteliers. He's allergic to the state of matrimony.'

'I'm beginning to think you are, too.'

'You're probably right, Tom.' She changed the subject.

'I'll have to get an appointment for a facial before that interview. I wouldn't want my stress lines to show for something that important.'

'Just threaten to cancel the shop's lease if they don't fit you in.'

'Tom, are you sure it's only Henry who has Mob connections?'

Tom just grinned. 'If you've finished pushing that omelette around on your plate to make me think you are eating, let's go.'

As they came out on to the pavement, Tom looked down the street and said, 'Shall we cut over to Michigan Avenue? It'll be easier to pick up a cab.'

'I wouldn't mind walking the whole way. It isn't so beastly hot tonight, and I could use the exercise.'

'In those shoes?' Tom looked doubtfully at the thin white straps which constituted Elizabeth's sandals, and shrugged. 'If you say so. Just cry uncle when you can't go on.'

'I'll bet I can outwalk you. I've been trying to do two miles in Grant Park every day.'

'The way you've been pacing, you probably do two miles in your office every day. Besides, I never bet on a sure thing.' They strolled a block, and Tom said, 'Did Mr Englin warn you about this reporter?'

'No. Should I be warned?'

'I don't think you've run into him before, but I have. He's scrupulously accurate with his facts, but one of his tricks is to wear his subject down and use a lot of subtle flattery and then throw out a pointed question while you're off guard.'

'That sounds like just the kind of fun I need, the mood I've been in lately.'

They turned on to Michigan Avenue. Across the street the two bronze lions guarding the front entrance of the Art Museum regarded them impassively.

'You have been saying what you think this week. It might not be wise with him around.'

'Maybe I'll just come down with a slight case of leprosy. You'll do fine with the interview.'

'Nope. I told you—I wouldn't look good on the grand staircase in an evening gown.'

'Especially with the beard.' Elizabeth laughed and reached up to rub her knuckles against the soft dark bristles.

Tom captured her hand and held it gently against his cheek. 'Elizabeth,' he pleaded. 'Am I insane to hope that someday you will see me as more than a friend?'

Elizabeth sighed. 'I'm fond of you, Tom.'

'But you don't love me.'

'No. I don't love anyone—anyone except Jeremy and Myles.'

'And him.'

'Who?' Elizabeth was startled.

'Your husband. That's why you're still so messed up over him. You've never stopped loving him.'

She shook her head. 'No. No, I don't love him any more.'

'Then why have you locked yourself away from the possibility of loving someone else? You won't even say his name. Why is that, if it isn't because you still love him?'

'Maybe it's because I hate what he did to me.'

Tom shook his head. 'I don't think so. But in any case, as long as you have half of your heart tied up in him—love or hate—you aren't free to care for anyone else.'

'Tom, we're making a spectacle of ourselves. We are standing on Michigan Avenue, after all.' She tried to walk on.

He wouldn't let her go. 'If it was him, you wouldn't care. I don't know if you'd be kissing him or screaming at him, but you wouldn't give a damn if you were on Michigan Avenue or standing in the middle of that fountain.' He gestured angrily across the street towards Buckingham Fountain, where the water, as if in answer, gushed a hundred feet in the air and the coloured light shifted to oranges and golds.

'I don't believe this. You are jealous of a ghost!'

'He's no ghost. Not to you. Elizabeth, I love you. But I cannot share you with a man who's been out of your life for years—a man who left because he enjoyed being cruel to you.'

'Nobody is asking you to share me.' Elizabeth tore away from his hands and started down the street.

He quickly caught up with her. 'Elizabeth, wait. That wasn't what I meant. . .'

A cruising cab pulled up at the stoplight, and Elizabeth hailed it. They rode the few blocks to the Englin in silence. At the entrance, she pulled a bill from her handbag. Tom protested.

'I hailed the cab, I'll pay for it,' Elizabeth said curtly and handed the bill to the cabby.

In the lobby, Tom said, 'Elizabeth, please. . .'

'I don't want to talk to you, Tom.' She punched the call button to summon an elevator.

'The truth hurts, doesn't it?' he said, and turned on his heel.

She stared after him, all of the anger suddenly drained out of her body. An elevator came, and a subdued Elizabeth rode up to the twenty-third floor.

Elizabeth sat cross-legged in the middle of the Carlisle's living room, carpet samples scattered around her. She looked from a rust-coloured swatch to the wide windows facing out over the Loop and half closed her eyes to see the effect. Yes, that was it, she decided, and tagged the sample, putting it with the drapery fabric she had already chosen. Next week she'd take the samples and begin looking for furniture.

She was tired out, she told herself. Normally she enjoyed choosing colours and fabrics for the apartments, but today she just wanted to get done with the job. She tried to tell herself that it had nothing to do with the fact that the Carlisle and the Maxwell shared an entrance hallway. She was getting tired of seeing Grady every time she turned around, and she wasn't looking forward to his party tomorrow. She looked at her wristwatch and sighed. Another hour or so and he'd be home—she'd have to get off the penthouse floor. But at least when they were among a group at the party he'd have to be careful what he said.

She wondered briefly if he'd enjoyed having dinner with Vicki and Josh Andrews. It would have been fun to be a mouse in the corner just to watch Anne's technique.

The house phone rang. She stacked a few more samples and got to her feet. She wished she dared ignore it.

'Mrs Englin?' Jill asked. 'Mr Bradford asked me to call and tell you that Corbin Evans is here. Do you want to come down or shall I ask him to come up?'

'Send him up,' she said, and thought that the least Tom could have done would have been to call her himself.

It had been two days since their argument, and he hadn't given her an opportunity to patch up their friendship. Perhaps that was just as well, she thought; the longer he stayed angry at her, the more likely he was to accept the fact that she would never feel anything more than friendship for him. But it still hurt to lose a friend. She should have been more careful not to let him get serious about her. Tom could be stubborn; that was something she'd learned long ago.

And so could Corbin Evans. Why did his schedule have to bring him to Chicago just now? she wondered distractedly, stacking the rest of the fabric samples into a neat pile. At least she could put a good face on it, she told herself as she went out to the elevators. And Corbin was good company, most of the time.

The door to one of the elevators opened and Elizabeth stepped forward, but it was a woman who got out, an older woman in a neat print housedress with a sack of groceries in each arm. She nodded politely to Elizabeth and started for the service door of the Maxwell, fumbling for a key. As she reached the door, one of the bags tilted dangerously, and a head of lettuce and a carton of sour cream bounced on the carpet. Elizabeth was beside the woman in an instant, taking the bulging bag.

'Bless you,' the woman said. 'If I'd dropped that sack—'

Elizabeth stole a glance into it and had to agree. She could see two dozen eggs and a glass bottle of something. Inwardly she shuddered at the mess that would have had to be cleaned out of the carpet. 'No trouble at all.'

The woman glanced curiously from Elizabeth's jeans and Paisley-printed shirt to the open door of the Carlisle. 'Aren't you Mrs Englin?'

'Yes.'

'I'm Mr Logan's housekeeper. I thought it must be you—but I never expected to see you in jeans.'

'The grapevine, no doubt? I'm glad to see it's wrong once in a while.'

The housekeeper nodded. 'There's a terrible gossip-mill around this place, isn't there?'

'Everyone always knows what you're having for breakfast before it's even cooked. Worse yet, they always know who's having breakfast with whom.'

'I'll tell Mr Logan to watch out,' the woman said dryly.

Elizabeth added hastily, 'Not that I care who Mr Logan's having breakfast with, or if it hits the grapevine. I was just using the example.' It hadn't seemed to surprise the housekeeper, though. Elizabeth wondered just who Grady was having breakfast with.

The elevator door opened again and Corbin nearly

smothered her with a bear hug. He draped an arm around her shoulders and walked her back to the Carlisle.

'Myles has your nose back to the grindstone, hmm? I can't say that I approve of the costume. Most women look lousy in jeans. Why don't you run out to Los Angeles next week and play for a few days?'

'I can't. Too many things to do.'

'Tom Bradford told me that Jeremy is in Wisconsin. So you're free.'

Elizabeth raised an eyebrow. 'Did Tom volunteer the information?'

Corbin grimaced. 'No. I had to use a crowbar. I'd like to know what that guy has against me.'

'He's jealous of you.'

'You're a little stuck on yourself, aren't you? What does he have to be jealous of? He certainly can't be doing any worse with you than I am.'

'Probably a little better,' Elizabeth agreed calmly. 'He's on the scene all of the time, you see.'

'I wish I could be. If you're not coming to L.A.—'

'I'm not.'

'I've got a marvellous new restaurant picked out for you. . .'

'Next year at convention time,' she parried easily.

'You're seriously wounding my pride, do you know that? I can't think of another woman I'd chase like this.'

'That's because most of them chase you. It's good for you to have a change now and then.'

'It doesn't sound as if it bothers you. Do I have other competition now?' Corbin asked suspiciously.

'I don't recall making any promises that you'd be the only man in my life. And I certainly don't remember your telling me I was the one and only woman.'

'Elizabeth, you know darned well I'm not getting married again. When a man has to live out of a suitcase as much as I do, it just doesn't work. But I think it's ridiculous for both of us to be unhappy for lack of a little love.'

Elizabeth folded her arms. 'What it comes down to, Corbin, is that you don't think a woman can be happy anywhere except in a man's bed. Now if you want a playmate in Chicago the way you have them lined up in every other city, I'll be happy to suggest some phone numbers. But don't hassle me.'

Corbin sighed. 'That's the hell of it, Elizabeth, you are beginning to make me think it could work out, despite my better judgment, which says I'd be a fool if I got married again.'

'Listen to your better judgment, Corbin,' she said sweetly. 'It's almost tea time.'

He wrinkled his nose. 'The sun is over the yard-arm. Can I have a drink instead? Do you have the place stocked?'

'No, but we can walk down one flight and relax.'

'Sounds good. I just flew in from San Antonio—you should see the Englin there.'

'Is the remodelling all finished?'

'It looks shinier than ever. I'll have the weekend to check out your competition up the street, and then I'll be off to New York. Are you sure you won't take pity on a travel-weary man? I won't be home till the end of the month.'

'No.'

'You're not sure?' He pulled the Carlisle's door shut behind them.

'Stop playing at romantics. And don't get the idea that I'm holding out for marriage. If you proposed right now I'd push you down the fire stairs.'

'Don't bother to be subtle, Elizabeth. Where shall we have dinner tonight?' His voice was husky, and he stopped her at the bottom of the stairs to nuzzle the nape of her neck.

'Cut it out. I'm not going out tonight. Jeremy will be back in a couple of hours, and I'm going to spend the evening with him.'

'Leave him with Florence.'

'Not on his first evening at home.'

'How about dinner tomorrow?'

'Don't you ever get discouraged? I have an engagement.'

'Break it.'

'I wish I could. Not for your sake, either. Next time give me a little warning; you must know that I'm a busy woman. But you can come to the Chicago League's dance tomorrow if you have the hundred bucks admission charge.'

'Do you promise to dance with me or is that extra?' Corbin asked.

Myles came in as she was pouring drinks, and sat down to talk to Corbin. Elizabeth sipped her Manhattan and listened to the conversation, putting in a comment here and there. She was frequently surprised by how good a grasp Myles retained on the hotel business, considering that it had been six years since he'd been active in it. Not only did he know every numeral on the Englin's balance sheet, but he could still recite the profit margins of every Englin across the country.

'How did the work go on the Carlisle today?' Myles asked.

Elizabeth wrinkled her nose. 'Slow. I think I'll do it in rust and off-white.'

'Sounds stark,' Corbin commented, and got up to refresh his drink.

Myles ignored the interruption. 'Just don't get so decorator-happy that. . .'

The doorbell rang, and Elizabeth jumped up. 'That'll be Jeremy,' she said, and hurried towards the entryway.

'Never saw anybody so crazy about a kid,' Corbin muttered, and Myles gave him a disapproving look.

Elizabeth flung the front door open and said, 'Jeremy, darling! Welcome. . .' Her welcome broke off in the middle as she realised it was not Jeremy who stood there. 'Oh, it's you,' she said.

Grady straightened his tie. 'It's obvious who's more popular around here. Luckily, Myles invited us down, so we don't have to rely on your hospitality. Fortunate, isn't it?'

'For you. If it was up to me to invite you, I'd serve hemlock punch.'

'Maybe I should leave a letter to the homicide squad attached to my will, telling them who to look for if I die of unnatural causes,' Grady mused. 'Elizabeth, I'd like you to meet my brother Jared.'

A voice from deep in her memory assaulted Elizabeth. 'Rick was my brother's friend, not mine,' Grady had said. She summoned all the composure she possessed and held out a hand to the man who had been Rick's friend.

Jared Logan was a fraction of an inch taller than Grady, and perhaps a little broader shouldered. There was no denying the likeness between them, Elizabeth thought, for their faces were the same shape and the expression in their eyes identical—distrustful, she told herself wryly. All she needed was to have a pair of cynics on her hands. But there the resemblance stopped, for Jared's hair was almost black where Grady's was brown and Jared's eyes were midnight-blue instead of his brother's brilliant sapphire. And Jared wore a small dark moustache. It made him look a bit like a Spanish *caballero*.

She was getting an inquiring look, and she realised abruptly that she hadn't the vaguest idea of what had been said. She must have been standing there like a teenager suffering from her first crush.

'Are you going to let us come in?' Grady asked impatiently, in the tone of a man who isn't used to asking for something twice.

'Do I have a choice?' Elizabeth drawled.

'No. Oh, Jared, this charming creature here, the one with such ladylike manners, is the general manager of this place,' Grady snapped.

Elizabeth gave him a blinding smile and turned to lead the way back into the apartment.

Myles was delighted to meet another son of his good friend. Corbin wasn't as happy, until he heard the name Logan. But Elizabeth heard only the fringes of the conversation. As she had expected, it was only a few minutes until Grady, a Scotch and soda in one hand and a bacon-wrapped appetiser in the other, sat down beside her.

'You don't look very happy,' he observed.

'I'd be a lot happier if you weren't here.'

'I'm not your guest, Elizabeth, I came to see Myles. Of course, when Jeremy arrives, I'll be paying particular attention to you. I'd hate for him to think you were lonely here at home while he played.' He crunched the appetiser and smiled appreciatively. 'I wonder what shade of purple he'll turn when he comes in to find his favourite lady with three eligible men?'

'I don't imagine he'll worry. But perhaps you should. He still bites sometimes when his favourite toy is taken away.' Elizabeth walked across the room and pretended to be selecting an appetiser. She was still staring at the stuffed olives when Jared Logan reached for a titbit.

'I don't believe we've met before, have we, Elizabeth?' he asked.

'No—no, we haven't.'

'I realise it's a long time ago, and that perhaps I shouldn't bring up the past, but I wanted to tell you how sad I was about Rick's death.'

'Thank you.'

'I knew him, you see—we were fraternity brothers.'

'Yes, I knew.' She had to find out—she had to be warned. 'How well did you know Rick?'

'Quite well.' Jared paused while he decided between cream cheese and pâté, then the midnight-blue eyes were intent on Elizabeth's face. 'Well enough to know Rick was never married, if that's what you're asking.'

She was mesmerised by those dark eyes, holding hers so she could not look away. For ten full seconds the silence reigned, and nothing around her had any reality. Then a delighted little voice screamed, 'Mommy!' and her son collided with her in what could have been called a tackle.

'Jeremy—baby,' she murmured, and she buried her face in his hair. Over the two fair heads, the brothers' eyes met, and Grady emptied his glass in a gulp.

Elizabeth tousled Jeremy's hair. 'Where's Tonya?'

'She's coming. She was so slow, I couldn't wait,' he explained. 'How are the fish?'

'They're fine. Florence has been feeding them every day. Let's go to meet Tonya.'

He shook his head positively. 'I'm going to see the fish.' They were always 'the fish' to Jeremy. Elizabeth wondered again, as she frequently had, why he'd never named them. Doubtless she could construct some deep-seated psychological reason if she tried hard enough.

Tonya was talking to Florence in the hall. Elizabeth gave her a hug. 'Come on in and have a drink, honey,' she invited. 'After a whole week of two five-year-olds, you must need it.'

Tonya shook her head. 'No—Brian's waiting in the car, pouting because he couldn't come up to play. Besides, when I tell you the bad news, you may never want to see me again.'

'Shall I sit down, or can I take it standing?'

'You know little Peter that the boys were playing with on Friday when you first arrived?'

'Yes.'

'He has chicken pox.'

'Oh, lord. What's the incubation period?'

'Fourteen to twenty-one days, according to my well-worn and probably outdated Dr Spock. We will be in suspense for another two weeks. Just about the time school starts. Isn't that my luck? The first minute I could get the kid off my hands every day he gets sick.'

'Alfred Hitchcock couldn't have planned it better, Tonya. Are you sure you don't need a drink?'

'No, I won't intrude on your guests.'

'Let me give it to you on the best of authority—they came to see Myles, not me.'

But Tonya just laughed and declined the invitation. 'Not when I look like this.' She indicated her hair, tied up in a red bandanna, and her cutoff jeans, which revealed long legs browned by a month of sunbathing.

'You look great and you know it.'

Tonya grimaced. 'I don't let Alan see me like this, you know. I didn't even want to walk through the lobby for fear someone would recognise me. I certainly am not going to compete with you when I've just had a four-hour drive.'

'What's so elegant about me? I'm wearing jeans.'

Tonya laughed. 'It's the atmosphere, Elizabeth. You always look elegant; the rest of us have to work at it. You're going to the League's dance tomorrow, aren't you?'

'I suppose so.'

'Taking Tom?'

'He isn't speaking to me. Corbin Evans is in town.'

Tonya frowned. 'That poor excuse for a male? We're going to have to see what we can do about you.'

'Please—spare me. Blind dates I don't need.'

'I'll argue that point with you someday. In the meantime, I'm double-parked, and even if I do get tired of

Brian, I'd hate to have the cops tow him off along with the car. Besides, it's Alan's car. I'll see you tomorrow.'

'Thanks, Tonya. Jeremy always enjoys it when he can stay with Brian.'

'Let me warn you, they were making all kinds of plans. That trip to the Cubs game the last time Brian stayed here has won you a friend for life.'

'Let me know the moment Brian breaks out.'

'I refuse to admit that it's possible. I'm going to use the power of positive thinking.'

Elizabeth was leaning against the front door trying to remember whether Jeremy had already had chicken pox during his checkered childhood when Corbin came down the hall.

'Since you aren't going out with me tonight, I guess I'll go do some work so whenever you're free I'll be available,' he said. 'I assume you can at least fit me in for nine holes of golf on Sunday?'

'Of course. The back nine at Lakewood?'

'Absolutely. And I'm going to beat you this time.'

'Care to bet?'

'Not this time.' He dropped a kiss on her cheek. 'As it happens, I invited the Logan brothers to join us.'

'You did what?'

Corbin looked surprised at her expression. 'I thought it was an ideal time to cultivate the acquaintance. It isn't every day that I get the chance to get close to two Logans at the same time, and it would be handy to have a friend in the organisation next time we're looking for a loan.'

'With friends like the Logans, you'd be better off with Honest Abe the loan shark.'

'What's wrong with you, Elizabeth? You're not the same person.'

'I don't want to spend a morning on a golf course with Grady and Jared Logan.'

'Elizabeth, more business is done on golf courses than

in boardrooms.' Then Corbin gave up. 'All right. Whatever you say. I'll get us out of it somehow.'

'Either you do, or I get sick,' she threatened.

'I've already said I'll handle it. Will I see you tomorrow before the dance?'

'Probably, sometime.'

'Well, that's some encouragement,' Corbin said. He kissed her and let himself out.

Elizabeth put a hand over her eyes and sighed. 'Of all the things I don't need. . .' she moaned.

'I can tell you something you do need,' Grady said cheerfully. 'An appointment book to keep all your men apart. Do they always fall over each other like this?'

Elizabeth ignored him and started down the hall.

Grady fell into step behind her. 'He's on the terrace—at least I assume you're looking for your son and heir?'

Elizabeth kept walking.

'Obviously, you're very attached to him,' Grady mused. 'I wonder—is it because he's all that lets you hang on to your position here? It would certainly account for how devoted Myles is to you. Or is it because he's all that is left of Rick?'

Elizabeth stopped in midstep. There was no more than the usual current of sarcasm in Grady's voice—had Jared not told him that Rick had not been married?

'Or is he even Rick's?' that smooth voice speculated.

'I am tired of being accused of two-timing Rick,' Elizabeth said harshly. 'If you jump to conclusions in the bank as you do in your personal life, I feel sorry for the business!'

He was silent for two paces. 'You didn't answer the question.'

'How clever of you to notice.'

'Don't you even know who your son's father is?'

Elizabeth clenched her hands until her nails bit into

skin. 'Yes, I know. And I can't see that it's any possible business of yours.'

'Can't you? But I can. From the age he appears to be, he could even be mine.'

'Don't jump to conclusions. You were in Bridgedale at the end of July. Jeremy was born the following January 28th—I'll show you his birth certificate if you like. And if you think that adds up to nine months you'd better give up finance for a career in the law.'

Grady's hand shot out and whirled her around to face him. 'You little tramp! You were already pregnant when we were together?'

'Yes, I was.'

'Were you looking for some poor stooge who'd believe your ten-pound child was premature?' His voice lashed out like a whip. 'How unfortunate for you that I slipped out of your trap. I'd have been easier to convince. But you just started all over, didn't you? And Rick Englin turned out to be the lucky man. Did the poor sucker ever know he'd given his name to another man's child?'

'Have you considered writing soap operas? I'd say you've a natural talent.' Elizabeth's breathing was a bit faster than normal; otherwise she was perfectly assured.

'Oh, what a bedtime story this would make for Myles.'

'You'd kill him. And then I'd have a better story for Whit. Can you prove you're not Jeremy's father? Doctors can be bribed, you know. I could find a couple who'd swear he was born prematurely. It would give Whit's ulcer a year's food for thought if he was told the son he's so proud of had a child by a hotel maid.' She tore free from his suddenly loosened grip and went out on to the terrace.

CHAPTER FIVE

JEREMY perched on his knees on a chair beside Elizabeth's dressing table, elbows propped on the glass top, painstakingly observing as she made up her face.

'You've got too much stuff on your cheeks,' he said. 'Why do you put all that gunk on, anyway?' He looked at her closely. 'To hide your puffy eyes?'

Elizabeth sighed and put the make-up case down. If her attempt to disguise recently-shed tears couldn't fool her five-year-old, how could it escape the eyes at Grady's party? Or at the League's dance afterwards.

'Why did you cry?'

'There are a lot of reasons why we cry, Jeremy. Sometimes we don't even know ourselves.'

The little boy nodded sagely. 'I cry sometimes. But I know why.'

'Because you're hurt?' Elizabeth picked up the eyebrush again. It was worth another try. She studied her face and brushed on more green eyeshadow. That helped. It made her eyes look big and mysterious, not as if they were about to overflow with tears.

'No, that's not why I cry.' He was silent a moment, as if wondering if he'd already said too much. Elizabeth shot an enquiring look at him, and he blurted out, 'Because I want my father to come back.'

'Oh, Jeremy.' Elizabeth pulled him close, as if, by shielding him in her arms, she could hold away all the hurts. He buried his face in the soft knit at the gathered neckline of her ivory dress.

'Why don't I have a father like Brian does?' he asked.

It was not the first time he had asked. A wave of

memory assailed Elizabeth—the laughter and the joy she had shared with Jeremy's father. And then the utter desolation of loss settled over her like a fog. 'He went away, Jeremy.' It was pitifully inadequate, but she didn't think he was able to accept the whole story. She certainly wasn't able to tell him yet.

'Why did he go away?'

'Because there were other things more important to him than we were.'

Jeremy's chin wobbled and Elizabeth drew him closer. 'Sometimes I hate him because he went away. He hates me, or he wouldn't have.'

'No, dear. He didn't hate you. And you shouldn't hate him. Jeremy, sometimes it's better for everybody if the mother and the father don't try to stay together. It's better if they're apart than if they're arguing all of the time.'

Jeremy raised his head from her shoulder. 'Brian's mom and dad argue sometimes,' he pointed out defiantly.

'Everybody argues sometimes. Brian's mother and father love each other very much. Brian's a lucky boy.'

'Didn't you love my father?'

She had put her foot in it again. How easy it all was to a child, before the simple blacks and whites got stirred up into all the shades of grey!

'I thought I did. I was very young, Jeremy. I'm not sure I knew what love was.'

Jeremy looked disgusted. Elizabeth couldn't blame him. The explanation sounded a little lame to her, too. But it was true—she had been young, and she had thought she loved him, and she didn't quite know how she felt about it all now, with a few years' perspective. The soul-ache she still felt each time she was reminded of him—was that love? or was it just that she felt sorry for herself? Did she miss what they had shared? or only what she had wanted to believe they had shared?

She was still thinking about that as she tapped on the

door of the Maxwell at one minute past seven. But she dismissed it as the door was opened. She would need all her mind to avoid the twin pitfalls of Grady and Jared, and who knew what dangers lay in the other invited guests?

The butler—tall, correct, white-haired—showed her into the drawing room she remembered so well. The harvest colours she had chosen so carefully, the deep yellows, the golds, the browns, were highlighted by the paintings Grady had added. She wondered briefly if he had bought them to suit the room or if he had already owned them. There wasn't a piece there that a museum would have turned down. Mostly American artists; all good ones. An Edward Hopper landscape, all angular shadows, hung above the fireplace. It was certainly an improvement on the reproduction she had put there when she redecorated.

Elizabeth's eyes swept over the room. Jared Logan was beside the fireplace with a girl in vivid red—Anne Andrews, with her fondest wish realised, Elizabeth thought. Vicki was curled into a comfortable chair near the fireplace with Josh perched on the arm. Elizabeth wondered how Vicki had managed to be there. Well, it was none of her business. Chances were, Grady had done the inviting all by himself.

He was at the bar. 'Hello, Betsy,' he said. 'Can I get you a drink?'

'Please. Just white wine.'

He raised an eyebrow. 'No Manhattans tonight?'

'I only drink those when I know I can trust the company.'

He laughed. 'I'm glad to know that. Obviously you do trust Corbin.'

Anne excused herself and fluttered across the room to hang on Grady's arm. He shifted Elizabeth's glass to the other hand just in time, and handed it to her.

'It's so nice to have you here this evening,' Anne purred. Under the smooth voice, Elizabeth heard a note of challenge, and the girl's eyes were anything but welcoming.

'I'm very pleased to be here,' Elizabeth murmured. Grady was really robbing the cradle now, to ask Anne to be his hostess at a party. Vicki must have had a hand in this, she decided. Despite her age, however, Anne was a fast learner. And she obviously had plans for Grady's future, and wished to make that fact plain to Elizabeth.

The butler ushered another couple into the room. With a last pat on Grady's sleeve, Anne went to greet the new arrivals. Elizabeth saw them and sighed in relief. Tonya and Alan McConnell—at least she had a couple of friends in the room. Suddenly, she stopped to consider. She herself had introduced Grady to Vicki and Josh, and to Alan. He couldn't possibly have had this party planned at the beginning of the week!

'Anne seems to be getting into the spirit of the thing,' she murmured. 'Charming child, isn't she? All of nineteen now.' And she raised limpid eyes to meet Grady's. 'Are you thinking of getting married?'

'As a matter of fact, yes.'

'The merger of the fortunes—I can see the headlines now. And the vows—you'll have to write special ones. "I, Grady, take thee, Anne, and thy father's bank stock, to be my lawful shareholder, to live together after John Maynard Keynes' holy ordinance. . ."'

'Cut it out, Elizabeth. You're not very charming when you're being catty.'

'Did I have the right variety of economist there? I'd hate to have chosen the wrong philosophy. Have you checked it out with your father yet? Though I don't imagine he could object. Anne's an only child, and Josh controls a big proportion of that bank. It would give Whit an opening I'm sure he couldn't refuse.'

'I don't plan to ask Whit's permission. I am thirty years old.'

'Are you sure that's wise?' Elizabeth asked. 'It would be foolish to risk his disapproval. But then, I'm sure he'll be delighted. It would be a shame to waste the opportunity to consolidate the family holdings, so to speak.' She sipped her wine. 'And to think we were so worried about his plans for us. Beside a banking heiress, what do I have to offer?'

Grady looked at her quizzically. 'Sarcasm doesn't fit you well, Betsy.'

'But I'm not being sarcastic,' Elizabeth protested. 'When is the happy day?'

'All right, you two, stop hiding in corners,' Josh Andrews boomed, and Vicki chimed in, 'Liz, I wanted to ask you if Tuesday would be a good day for us to have lunch and talk about the arrangements for the ball.' She linked her arm into Elizabeth's and led her away from the bar.

'That would be fine, Vicki,' Elizabeth said, thinking an unladylike word. She had originally suggested Tuesday; now Vicki was coming back to it as if it were her own idea. Who cares? she tried to tell herself. As long as the results are good, what does it matter which day we have lunch? 'You must have the dance arrangements well under control to be here.'

Vicki shrugged. 'One has to eat somewhere. And Grady is such a dear boy. I'm so glad we didn't have to miss his party. Anne would have been heartbroken.'

I'll bet, Elizabeth thought.

'Isn't he the most handsome young man you've ever met?'

'Grady? No.' Elizabeth sipped her wine.

Vicki looked shocked, but she didn't pursue the subject. 'Hasn't he done a marvellous job of decorating?'

Elizabeth nearly dropped her glass. But Vicki, she saw with a sideways glance, was serious. 'Oh, yes,' Elizabeth drawled. 'The colour scheme is lovely. I wonder how he thought of it. Just what I would have chosen myself.'

'And such good taste in art. That Hopper piece must have cost him a fortune.'

There Elizabeth found herself able to agree whole-heartedly. Grady did have good taste in art. Or his decorator did, she told herself cynically.

'Is Grady's brother a banker, too?'

'No. But I don't know what he does. Why don't you ask him?'

'Maybe he's just enjoying life,' Vicki shrugged. 'Whitney Logan's boys shouldn't have to work at all.'

Elizabeth didn't answer that. There was an intensity about Grady that made her think of a coiled spring whenever she looked at him. He wasn't the kind who could enjoy just watching the panorama of life; he'd be right in there doing something—anything—doing it well and efficiently. There was a bit of the same quality about Jared, as though he were perpetually poised for action. She couldn't picture either of them whiling his life away on a yacht. On a sailboat, perhaps—manhandling the boat, facing the spray. . .

'Are you ready to go in to dinner?'

Elizabeth jumped. Jared was beside her, an eyebrow raised enquiringly.

She set her wineglass down and slipped a hand into the crook of his arm. 'Yes, of course. I must have been daydreaming. I've been a bit preoccupied lately.'

He didn't answer that, but the eyebrow went up a trifle farther and Elizabeth felt like a fool. Where was her poise? she scolded herself. For years, she had handled every crisis and maintained the cool aloofness that was her trade-mark. Now whenever she hit the slightest bump she was acting like a freshman co-ed. Somehow she had to get her balance back.

She sat between Jared and Alan, exchanging banter

with Alan. During the soup course, he said, with a glance at Grady, 'It just occurred to me that he must be the tenant you were trying to evict this week. Am I right?'

Elizabeth nodded.

'Obviously he didn't want to tear up the lease.'

'How'd you guess?'

'You do like to play with fire, don't you, Elizabeth?' he commented, and turned to Vicki Andrews.

Elizabeth kept her conversation with Jared light, never daring to say what was on her mind. Had he told Grady yet that Rick had died a bachelor? She didn't think so, for she was reasonably sure that Grady would have flaunted the knowledge as soon as she walked into the room. Yet she couldn't imagine why Jared wouldn't have told his brother right away.

Dinner dragged on, and it wasn't until they had returned to the drawing room that Elizabeth felt able to relax a little.

She watched Anne settle herself with a little confident flounce behind the coffee service, and allowed herself an instant of disgust. Even if Grady was planning to marry the girl, he ought to have had the sense not to ask her to be his hostess until the engagement was announced.

'You look as if you just bit into something sour,' Tonya said quietly as she sat down next to Elizabeth.

Elizabeth flicked a glance at Anne. Tonya followed it and nodded. 'I feel the same way,' she mused. 'Somebody ought to tell the girl not to count her chickens until the ring is on her finger—and I don't mean the diamond one.'

'Especially when it's Grady,' Elizabeth murmured.

Tonya shot a surprised look at her. 'You look a little crackled around the edges,' she observed. 'Something wrong?' When Elizabeth didn't answer, Tonya returned to the original subject. 'I'm not going to be the one who warns Anne, though,' she said. 'It just might teach her a lesson. And her mother, too, come to that.'

Elizabeth looked over at Vicki, who was making herself at home. 'I have it on the best of authority that it's serious.'

'If it came from Mama, I wouldn't consider her an authority.'

'It didn't. You're vice-president of the Chicago League this year, aren't you?'

Tonya groaned. 'Don't remind me.'

'Vicki's setting up the débutante ball for the Englin.'

'Good. It'll be like old times. Remember the year we had our début?'

'Yes. How excited we were, and how your mother used to threaten us that if we didn't act like ladies we'd be taken off the list.'

'I remember. She was still telling you that on the night of the ball when you took your shoes off in the receiving line.' Tonya giggled. 'I wish she could see you now—the perfect society leader, always cool and elegant, and absolutely never flustered.'

Tonya hadn't seen much of her in the last few days, Elizabeth reflected, if she still thought of her as never being flustered. But she dismissed the thought and remembered the night she had been a débutante. 'Poor Rick, he was almost as mortified as your mother,' Elizabeth reflected. 'He hated it so—all the society functions—just as I did, at the time. And Myles made him escort me to the ball. . .' She started to laugh, remembering some of the arguments Rick had advanced in an effort to escape.

'And you treated the poor guy like dirt all evening because you didn't want him to be there.'

'After all, I didn't want him following me around. Who could blame me if I treated him badly?'

'Who, indeed?' Grady said softly, and handed her a cup and saucer. 'It certainly wasn't the only time you treated him like dirt, was it, Betsy?' Then he was gone.

'What's the matter with him?' Tonya sputtered. 'Elizabeth, you're white. Oh, honey . . . what a rotten thing for him to say.'

'I think I need some fresh air.' Elizabeth clutched at her poise with the last of her strength. She set the cup down, illogically proud that her hand was rock steady. 'I'll be back in a few minutes.' She glanced around the room and slipped out the french doors, confident that only Tonya had seen her go.

She walked over to the terrace railing and looked out over the city. To the north lay the Golden Mile, the lights of restaurants and clubs brilliant in the gathering dusk. The Standard Oil building loomed, the sky not yet dark enough to absorb the outline of the skyscraper, yet dark enough that the lights inside the structure formed a jewelled necklace. Lake Michigan lay still and calm to the east. The sound of traffic came muted to her ears. Elizabeth sighed, and told herself firmly that sighing was a habit she'd have to break.

'Would you like some company?'

She turned quickly, and Jared came across the terrace. She saw the worried lines in his forehead relax as he studied her face.

'Were you afraid I was going to throw myself over the railing?'

'The thought occurred to me.'

Elizabeth shook her head firmly. 'I'm not the type. And if I was, I wouldn't do it here. It would be bad publicity for the hotel.'

He laughed. 'That sounds more like you. Don't let my crazy little brother upset you. He's something like a bulldog, you know; once he gets hold of an idea it takes TNT to get it away from him.'

'I'd noticed,' Elizabeth said dryly. She gazed over the lake for a moment. A plane took off from the small airfield and roared out over the marina. 'Why didn't you tell him I wasn't married to Rick?'

He was silent for a few seconds. 'I don't know, Elizabeth. I usually talk first and think about it later. But this time it occurred to me that it isn't any of my business if my brother wants to make a fool of himself.' He put his hand on top of hers on the railing. 'And if Myles isn't raising any fuss about the circumstances of Jeremy's birth, then I don't think it's any of my business or Grady's.'

It was strangely reminiscent of something Rick had said to her shortly after Jeremy was born: 'I think you're crazy, Elizabeth, but if you're convinced you're doing the right thing, then it isn't up to me to question you.' The aching loss swept over her again, and she turned blindly to the nearest comfort. 'I miss him so,' she murmured.

Jared put an arm around her. 'We all do, Elizabeth. He was a special person.'

She stood there for a couple of minutes soaking up the warmth of his concern, then laughed a little shakily and stepped away from him. 'I'm sorry. It isn't like me to throw myself at people I've just met,' she said.

He smiled. 'Would you like to be alone?'

She was grateful for his perception. 'Yes, I would, if you don't mind.'

'Only if you promise not to throw yourself overboard.' He gestured towards the railing.

'I promise. I told you—bad publicity for the hotel. Besides, I'd only fall one storey and land on my own terrace.'

They shared a laugh, and Jared went inside. Elizabeth turned again to the railing. A breeze stirred the loose tendrils of her hair.

'I see you've found another victim.'

Elizabeth didn't even jump. It was inevitable that Grady would have seen her with Jared. The man was omnipresent.

'I have to admit he'd be a better choice than Corbin. Jared owns a hundred per cent of the stock in his company. Nobody tells him what to do. If he wanted to, he could sign over the whole works to you tomorrow.' He came a little closer. 'That ought to save you some research time—are there any more questions you'd like answered?'

Idly, Elizabeth asked, 'What does Jared do?'

'He manufactures computers and other electronic equipment. I doubt you could handle it yourself, but you could always hire him to run the place after you con him out of it.'

Elizabeth turned away from the railing. 'What do you think I am—Mata Hari? If you'll excuse me. . .' She tried to brush past him.

Grady's hand shot out and caught her arm. 'I wonder what you would do if you came up against a man who wasn't blinded by your beauty. I wonder if it's too late to teach you to be a woman instead of a calculating siren. . .'

She saw his intention in his eyes, and protested faintly. But Grady paid no attention. He drew her close, moulding her slender body to his, his hands moving with deliberate care over the sensually smooth fabric of her dress.

'Don't do this, Grady.'

'Why not? Are you afraid of what you'll find out about yourself?'

She looked into his eyes for an instant, afraid of the smouldering desire she saw there.

He kissed her slowly, teasingly, then released her lips to let his mouth trail down her throat to the low neckline of her dress.

Elizabeth slapped him.

It was only a glancing blow, but there was fiery anger in his eyes. He seized her wrist and inexorably put it behind her back, capturing both of her hands with one of his. 'You'll pay for that, Betsy,' he said, and pulled her back with him into the shadow of a big potted plant. She struggled, but it was a one-sided battle, and in seconds she lay quiet in his arms. 'That's better,' he breathed against her lips, and Elizabeth wondered a little muzzily if she was going to faint.

The next few minutes seemed to last forever, and each kiss blasted holes in Elizabeth's poise, until she found herself returning kiss for kiss, standing on her toes to arch her body more closely against him. She didn't remember just when he had freed her hands, but her arms were around his waist under his jacket, her palms caressing the starched linen of his formal shirt as if it had been his skin. Shocked at her own behaviour, Elizabeth pulled away. This time Grady let her go, his hands sliding reluctantly over the smooth skin of her almost-bare back, and stepped back a pace, straightening his tie and rebuttoning his jacket.

Elizabeth put her hands up to her hair, feeling tendrils coming loose all over her head. She would have to make some repairs before she dared go back into the drawing room, she thought vaguely. Then she heard the approach of voices.

'Are you sure he came out this way?' Jared drawled. 'I didn't see him leave.'

'He must be here somewhere,' Anne said a little peevishly. 'It's really bad of him to walk out on his guests this way. We have to hurry or we'll be late for the dance.'

'He probably just needed a breath of air. Why don't you go around that side, and I'll look over here?'

Grady grinned. 'That's my brother—saving my neck. Good old Jared.'

'I hope she slits your throat!' Elizabeth flashed, and turned to dart through the darkened dining room. Before she was inside, though, she heard Jared say, 'Having fun?'

'Oh, yes,' Grady answered. 'How do you always know where to find me?'

'Simple. I just think about where I'd be under the circumstances. You're always there.'

Elizabeth didn't wait to hear more. She stood for a second in the dining room, wishing she had a mirror with her. She had no idea if she could pass inspection if someone saw her before she got to the powder room. 'You're too old to be snatching kisses at parties,' she scolded herself. But, in all honesty, it wasn't her fault if she was tousled.

She opened the dining room door cautiously and slipped down the long hall towards the bedrooms. Any of them would do to fix herself up before she returned to the party. She would just make sure to avoid the master suite.

She was halfway down the hall when the door of the small cloakroom opened and the butler came out with an armful of lacy shawls that the women guests had worn. It took every ounce of Elizabeth's self-control to nod politely at him rather than duck her head and run.

The butler had more poise. He didn't turn a hair at her appearance, just indicated the door of the powder room and continued down the hall. Elizabeth looked into the mirror in the powder room and groaned. It took her almost fifteen minutes to get her hair smoothed back into the upswept twist and reanchor the small spray of white daisies which highlighted the style. She was repairing her make-up when Tonya came in, fussing with her silk shawl.

'What's taking you so long?' she demanded. 'First we lose you and then Grady disappears. . . Me and my big mouth.'

'Don't add one and one and come up with three, Tonya,' Elizabeth advised.

'At least you have your colour back,' Tonya said unrepentantly. 'So tell me about Grady Logan.'

'There's nothing to tell.'

'I just can't figure you two out. One minute you're

throwing insults at each other and the next you're kissing on the terrace.'

Elizabeth shot a look at her friend.

Tonya shrugged. 'You must have been. Your hair isn't quite right yet.'

'I wasn't kissing him. He was kissing me.' Elizabeth was uncomfortably aware that she wasn't telling the truth.

'Of course, that explains everything,' Tonya drawled. 'Well, whenever you get around to talking about it, I'll be there. You missed a good show, too. While you were gone Vicki gave the best impression of a mother-in-law-in-waiting that I've ever seen. It was so blatant even Anne was trying to get her to shut up.' She eyed Elizabeth, who was unconcernedly applying mascara, and added, 'It was too much of a temptation to tell her that her prospective son-in-law had another woman in his arms at that very moment.'

Elizabeth cracked. 'You didn't!'

'No. But Anne knew it. You have an enemy there, my dear.'

Elizabeth shrugged. 'Anne I can handle. It's Grady I. . .'

'What is the deal with you and Grady?' Tonya begged. When Elizabeth remained silent, she sighed. 'All right, you win. Let's go.'

The League's officers and their escorts had already formed a receiving line by the time Elizabeth's group reached the Grand Ballroom. Beside Vicki was Anne, who was the president of the group of one hundred girls who had had their débuts at last year's ball. Beside Anne was Grady. The dark-haired girl was all smiles as she presented each person to him.

'Maybe I have it all wrong,' Tonya announced suddenly as she stopped on the threshhold of the ballroom, her hand tightening on Alan's sleeve. 'Maybe Vicki's after him herself. Maybe she's just using Anne as bait.' Then, abruptly, she remembered who was within hearing distance. 'Sorry, Jared. I didn't mean to imply anything. . .'

Jared laughed lazily. 'If my little brother makes a fool of himself over a woman, it won't be the first time. Or, no doubt, the last.' He looked down at Elizabeth and tightened his grip on her hand. There was a warning in his eyes.

'Don't worry about me,' she said demurely. 'I've run into his kind before.'

He didn't answer, but Elizabeth thought she could read doubt in his dark eyes. She looked around the room. The room was filling rapidly; it would be packed before midnight. Already the dance floor was crowded. The great crystal chandeliers were dimmed to create a romantic atmosphere for the dancers, and the high ceiling was thrown into shadow. Brightly-coloured lights danced around the band. The music shifted to a slow tempo, and Jared drew her on to the dance floor.

Elizabeth heard herself saying, 'What you said about Grady and his history with women—you aren't like him, are you? You don't make a fool out of yourself over any woman, do you?'

'Never. I've never yet met a woman I'd want to look at over the breakfast table for the next three days, much less thirty years. Thinking about it in those terms makes life much more comfortable.'

'That's definite. I do hope I'm around when you eat your words.'

He grinned. 'Under that cool sophistication, you're a romantic, aren't you, Elizabeth?'

'You don't leave anyone any illusions, do you? Even the romantics. You needn't fear anything from me, by the way. You're not my type.'

'What is your type?'

'I'm really not sure. Grady would tell you that my type is anyone who owns a blue-chip stock. Did you know he's planning to break the family tradition and be married?'

'I suspected it. I'm delighted.'

'You like her, then?' Elizabeth asked.

'It's got nothing to do with her. I presume you mean the teenaged terror? No, it's just that Mother can start hinting to him about grandchildren, and perhaps she'll leave me alone.' The band picked up the tempo again and they left the dance floor. 'Will it bother you if he marries Anne?'

Elizabeth laughed lightly. 'Why should it bother me? He only moved in a week ago. Why does everyone think there's something going on.'

'Because something is,' Jared said bluntly as he pulled out her chair.

Tonya leaned forward as he sat down. 'Did Grady tell me you build computers, Jared?'

Elizabeth only half listened to the answer. Out on the dance floor Anne and Grady were dancing, very close, very slowly. Her dark head rested confidently on his shoulder, the vivid red of her dress brilliant against the sober black of his evening clothes. Elizabeth watched, and sighed without realising.

'Tired?' Alan shifted his chair closer. Elizabeth looked up, startled. Tonya and Jared were gone.

'Oh, a little, perhaps. I took Jeremy to the zoo this afternoon, and I wore out a lot faster than he did. I must be getting old fast.'

'I just wish you could find that much time for me,' Corbin Evans said as he pulled out a chair and dropped into it.

'I didn't think you'd care to go.'

'To the zoo? Of course not, especially with the brat thrown into the bargain,' Corbin said flatly.

Out of the corner of her eye, Elizabeth saw Alan's

eyebrows go up. He didn't comment, though, just took a healthy swallow from the glass at his elbow.

'Let's go and dance. You don't mind, do you, Alan?' Corbin's question was rhetorical. He was already pulling Elizabeth to her feet as he spoke.

Out on the floor, she said, 'Corbin, there was no need to be rude.'

'I wasn't rude, I'm just jealous. I paid a hundred bucks for the privilege of dancing with you, so why shouldn't I be able to do it? The flowers in your hair are tickling my nose, by the way.'

'Well, don't take them out or it'll all fall down.'

'Not a bad idea,' he said, rubbing his cheek gently against her hair. 'Let's go out on the balcony and talk about it.'

'Let's not.' She glanced across the room, her eyes drawn as if by a magnet to meet Grady's. He was still dancing with Anne, even closer if that was possible, but his eyes were mocking as he met hers. Then she capitulated. 'All right. I need a breath of air. This room is getting too crowded.'

On the balcony overlooking the main lobby, Corbin drew her back into a secluded corner. His kiss was gentle, but when she remained unresponsive, he became more demanding. Then he broke off the embrace, saying angrily, 'What's the matter, Elizabeth? That was like kissing an ice cube.'

A few feet away someone coughed gently, and Elizabeth's backbone stiffened. She glanced over her shoulder to see Grady and Anne there. Anne was wearing a cold, catty smile, and Elizabeth had no doubt that this news would be broadcast as soon as Anne had an opportunity. She also had no doubt that Grady had carefully timed their arrival to occur at an embarrassing moment.

'How about changing partners?' Grady suggested

easily. 'Corbin, take pity on poor Anne here; she's been dancing with me all evening and she'll be labelled a wallflower if nobody else claims her.' He smiled down at her to take the sting out of the words, but Elizabeth saw sparks flare in Anne's big brown eyes. This had no place in Anne's scheme, that was obvious; she'd be delighted to be Grady's only partner.

'Of course,' Corbin said as graciously as he could, and they went back into the ballroom.

Elizabeth stifled a desire to giggle. 'That was unfair,' she accused. 'You knew quite well that neither of them can stand the other.'

'Did I?' he asked idly. He was watching her mouth, as if fascinated by its shape.

'And you also knew that Corbin wouldn't do anything to offend you because of who you are.'

'Shameless of me, isn't it?'

'I think you were taking advantage of me this week. Anybody who can be escorting the deb's president, within three days of meeting her, doesn't need my help.'

'But it was you who introduced me to her. You disappoint me, though, Betsy.'

'I'm not surprised. What have I done now?'

'I've been investigating Corbin Evans today. He sounds like a good prospect for you.'

'I consider him the second string on my bow. What you told me about Jared fascinated me, so, I think I'll try for him.'

He grinned. 'Give up, darling. I warned him about you. And Jared has never let the idea of marriage cross his mind.'

'Who said anything about marriage?' Elizabeth said sweetly.

It rocked him for a split second, then he regained his balance. 'Let's not quarrel about your chances with my brother. We'd never reach agreement. What really fascinates me is that—if Corbin is still on the second string— you can't do a little better at convincing him that he's irresistible. Kissing an ice cube, indeed. I didn't think I was kissing an ice cube upstairs a little while ago.'

'I wasn't expecting that. You took me by surprise.'

'Oh? And if you had been expecting it, you'd have given me the cold shoulder too? Let's try it out. You're expecting me to kiss you now, aren't you?' He didn't touch her, but he braced his hands against the wall she stood against, so that she couldn't move away.

She couldn't answer. She stared up at him like a frightened rabbit, knowing what he was going to do. And she knew that she couldn't pretend to be unmoved if he kissed her, any more than she had been able to up there on the terrace.

'Mrs Englin?' She was so absorbed that the bellboy had to repeat himself. 'Mrs Englin?'

Grady didn't move. Elizabeth turned her head against the gold-trimmed panel of the wall and said, 'Yes?'

'Mr Bradford sent me to ask you to come down to the Library Lounge. There's a policeman down there making a fuss; there seems to be something minor wrong with the drink licences.'

'Tell him I'll be right there.'

The bellboy touched his cap and ran down the grand staircase.

'Isn't that what you pay Bradford for? Or are you afraid to stay here?'

'This is the kind of thing I get paid for,' Elizabeth said acidly. 'If you don't mind. . .'

'What if I do mind?' But Grady unhurriedly straight- ened up and let her step away from the wall. 'Do you need a bodyguard?'

'Not your sort. You'd get aggressive and we'd both land in jail.'

'Very well. I'll wait for you.'

'It won't hurt my feelings if you don't. I promise!' Elizabeth flung the words over her shoulder as she ran down the stairs.

CHAPTER SIX

ELIZABETH stifled a yawn and reached for the coffeepot, the sleeve of her jade-green satin robe, with its heavy lace trim, dragging across her placemat. Across the table Jeremy was consuming bacon and eggs, and she looked at him with brief disfavour before turning away from the sight. Myles, engrossed in his Sunday paper, reached for his coffee.

Elizabeth stirred sugar into her cup and took a sip.

Florence saw her as she brought in a tray of sweet rolls. 'What's the matter with you?' she asked unsympathetically. 'Too much to drink last night?'

'No. Not nearly enough,' Elizabeth retorted. She thought longingly of how peaceful her life had been last Sunday morning. Then, she had been sitting at Tonya's sunny kitchen table up in Bridgedale, nibbling fresh coffeecake, with never a thought of Grady Logan. Ah, what an easy, uneventful life was mine, she thought.

'I never heard of anybody getting a hangover from too little to drink,' Florence snorted.

'I do not have a hangover, Florence. I am suffering from lack of sleep.' Elizabeth's voice was sharper than she had intended.

Myles looked up intently. 'Did the dance last till late?'

'You might say that. It was still going strong when I came up at two in the morning.'

'Who was at Grady's party?' He folded the local news section and laid it aside, focussing his entire attention on Elizabeth.

She could have groaned aloud. All she wanted this morning was quiet and peaceful surroundings. Why had

she got out of bed, anyway? Here she was faced with a
five-year-old whose cereal was chosen for the noise it
made and a seventy-five-year-old who wanted all the
details about a party. She refilled her coffee cup. After all,
she told herself, who could blame Myles for his questions?
Being an invalid didn't mean that his mind had slowed
down. If anything, it was hungrier for information.

'Just Josh and Vicki Andrews and their daughter, and
the McConnells, and Jared and Grady,' she said.

'Do Josh and Vicki have a daughter?'

'She's nineteen. And from all indications, she'll be
living upstairs before the year is out. Thanks, Florence.'
Elizabeth reached for the plate of buttered toast the
housekeeper had just put on the table. 'Grady thought she
was fascinating.'

'So that's what has you upset this morning?' Myles
chuckled. 'Don't worry about it, Elizabeth. Grady's got
more sense than to fall for a teenager. He'll come around.'

'We'd quarrel if I told you what I thought about that.'

Jeremy spooned up the last of his cereal and said, 'Are
you playing golf today?'

'I'm supposed to.'

'With Corbin? I don't like him, Mom.'

Myles looked at the child approvingly. 'You're going to
develop a businesslike head on those shoulders yet, young
man. You're already a good judge of character.'

'Better than I am?' Elizabeth asked dryly. 'I'm only
playing golf with the man, not marrying him.'

Jeremy ignored the byplay. 'Why don't you take me
somewhere instead?'

'You went to the zoo yesterday. You can caddy for me, if
I decide to golf.'

'Not if you're going with Corbin.' Jeremy's voice was
uncompromising. How very much he reminded her of his
father sometimes, Elizabeth thought with a pang.

'I did tell him I'd go.'

'So tell him you promised me instead.'

'I promised him first,' Elizabeth pointed out.

'Then tell him. . .' Jeremy's spoon was suspended while the big blue eyes stared out the window. 'Tell him you'd rather stay with me because he's boring. He is, you know. He's a wet blanket.'

Elizabeth laughed. 'A diplomat you'll never be,' she said.

Myles said, 'He's going to run the hotel, Elizabeth.'

She faced him squarely. 'Only if he wants to, Myles. You know how I feel about that. He isn't going to be forced into anything, the way. . .' She stopped suddenly.

'Like Rick was?' Myles asked softly. 'Like you were?'

'That wasn't what I meant, Myles, and you know it. Rick was happy, and I . . . I love the Englin. It's my life.'

'Then it shouldn't be, my dear.' Grey eyes met green ones and held them.

Elizabeth gave up. Myles would never be convinced that she was happy with the way things were—or had been happy, until Grady had shown up to threaten her peaceful existence.

Florence came back into the room. 'Mr Evans is on the phone, Elizabeth.'

Elizabeth turned at the doorway, the satin robe swishing about her feet, and came back to bend over Myles. 'I don't want to argue with you,' she said. 'I'm sorry.'

He smoothed the flaxen hair. 'I'm an old man, Elizabeth,' he said somberly. 'The world belongs to your generation now. We septuagenarians have to learn to stay out of it.' When she would have protested, he smiled and shooed her away. 'Go and answer your phone call, now.'

Corbin was impatient. 'I'd think, on Sunday morning, you'd be a little easier to find,' he complained. 'Can you be ready in an hour? The Logans are meeting us in the main lobby.'

Elizabeth started to do a slow burn. 'You said you'd get us out of that, Corbin,' she accused.

'Have you ever tried to un-invite somebody you don't want to offend?' Corbin pointed out. 'It's not easy. And Grady Logan must be among the most difficult.'

'I'll agree with that,' Elizabeth admitted.

'And I don't see what your complaint was, anyway. I've certainly played enough golf with your business associates.'

'You forget that they were invited so you could impress them,' Elizabeth muttered.

'I don't see why you won't go along with me this time. What harm can it do?'

'You'd be surprised.' She was thinking fast. Playing nine holes of golf with Corbin fawning over Grady, Grady taking every opportunity to needle her, and Jared overseeing the whole with a sardonic smile—the very thought was giving her a headache! 'Corbin, I'm just not up to golf with you and the Logans. Besides, Jeremy has made plans for today, and I really hate to disappoint him.'

'What about disappointing me? What am I supposed to tell them when they ask what happened to you?'

'They're intelligent men. Both of them can figure it out. But if they ask, which they probably won't, tell them I'm having a nervous breakdown this morning at eleven o'clock, and I don't want to miss it. See you later, Corbin.'

She put the telephone down hard and looked up to see Jeremy, a wide grin on his face, consuming the last of a sweet roll. 'Why didn't you tell him he was boring?' he asked. 'That would be the truth, and he wouldn't bother you any more.'

'Generally, he doesn't bother me, Jeremy. You're not supposed to be eating in here.'

Jeremy licked the frosting off his fingers. 'I'm not eating,' he pointed out reasonably. 'I'm finished. Where are you taking me today?'

'I'm sure you've already chosen the place.'

'Well, yes. The Museum of Science and Industry.'

'You were there just three weeks ago.'

'But that was with a whole bunch of kids, Mom, and I didn't get to do anything. And the submarine was too crowded to see anything. They made you walk through in a hurry.'

'Do you really think it'll be any better on a Sunday afternoon?' Elizabeth asked dryly.

'If we go right away. . .'

She groaned. 'Let me get dressed.' At least she'd be out of the hotel a good half-hour before Corbin told Grady that she wasn't golfing, Elizabeth told herself as she pulled canary-yellow slacks from her closet. And being in a crowd at a museum was better than having to sit around the apartment listening to Myles' philosophy on the rough course of true love. She completed her outfit with high-heeled sandals and a short-sleeved pullover in yellow and white stripes, caught her hair back with a canary-coloured scarf, and dabbed on lipstick. Jeremy wouldn't care if she didn't put on any make-up at all, but on second thoughts Elizabeth reached for the make-up kit. It was certain that when she went out looking less than her best, she inevitably met someone she needed to impress. She put the finishing touches on her make-up, tucked sunglasses into her handbag and went back to the dining room.

Jeremy was kneeling on a chair, watching intently as Grady sketched on a paper napkin.

'And that's why, if you look closely, all the pictures in the newspaper are really little dots,' Grady said and tossed his pen down.

Jeremy thoughtfully reached for another sweet roll. 'But if the newspaper can only print black. . .'

Elizabeth protested, 'Jeremy, if you eat another roll you're going to be sick.'

'Oh, Mom,' Jeremy wheedled. 'Not on Florence's rolls.'

They're too good.' He shot a sidelong glance at the housekeeper.

'If you think flattery will make me take your side, Counsellor, you're wrong,' she advised him. 'You're definitely going to be a lawyer. Another roll, Mr Logan?'

'If he can have another one,' Jeremy protested, 'why can't I?'

'Mind your manners,' Elizabeth warned. 'Are you ready to go, Jeremy?'

'In a little bit, Mom.' He returned to the attack. 'If they can only print black. . .'

'Have another cup of coffee, Elizabeth,' Grady advised. 'This may take a while.'

'No, thanks, Grady.'

'I'm delighted to find that I'm not invisible after all. I was beginning to think you couldn't see me.'

'Oh, I could see you. I was just hoping that if I ignored you, you'd go away.'

Myles looked up from the financial section. 'Now really, Elizabeth. . .' he protested.

'Jeremy says you're not playing golf today,' Grady observed.

'No, I'm not.'

'What an amazing coincidence. I'm not either. I can't, you see. Jared borrowed my clubs.'

'I'd have thought you would have learned to share your toys by now,' Elizabeth said acidly.

Grady merely smiled. 'So I'm at loose ends today. At least, I was until Jeremy invited me to go along to the Museum of Science and Industry.'

Elizabeth put both her hands on her hips and glared at him. Before she could speak, Grady had put a finger on his lips and directed a meaningful look towards Myles, who had turned back to his newspaper. So she merely sighed. He was right, she told herself. Myles was already a little suspicious of her attitude towards Grady. She'd better not make a scene.

'That was thoughtful of you, Jeremy,' she said instead, 'but I'm sure Mr Logan has other things he would rather do today. We must not tie up a whole day of his precious free time.'

'Not at all,' Grady said cheerfully. 'And Jeremy assures me I'll come in very handy because I can explain all these things to him. I think he's giving me credit for an awful lot of knowledge, but I'll try not to disappoint him.'

A bit desperate, Elizabeth tried again. 'Grady, you shouldn't let Jeremy talk you into anything. I'm sure you'd be bored silly out there today.' She waved a casual hand. 'I wouldn't want you to be bored.'

Grady's eyes sparkled disingenuously. 'Who could be bored, Betsy?' His eyes trailed down over her slender body, and it was several moments before he met her eyes again. But his voice was innocent. 'Jeremy assures me there's a real German submarine, and a whispering tunnel, and all kinds of computers. . .'

'Don't forget the coal mine.' Jeremy's voice was a bit indistinct, since he had—with everyone ignoring him—snagged his extra sweet roll after all. 'Come on, Mom. Don't talk him out of it. You know you hate all that machinery stuff.'

Elizabeth remembered, bitterly, what Corbin had told her a few minutes earlier—something about Grady being very hard to get rid of. It appeared that he was right.

'All right,' she said finally. 'But let's get going if you want to see that submarine before there's a queue.'

She was rewarded with two of the sweetest smiles in the city. Grady's didn't fool her, though, and when Jeremy turned his back for an instant, she hissed at the complacent man, 'You'd better not spoil that little boy's day at the museum with your tricks!'

'I promise I'll be the picture of fond avuncular attention. Or should I be practising my paternal air? Have you decided to tell Whit your fairy-tale about Jeremy being my kid?'

But the boy was back before she could retort.

The drive across town and down Lake Shore Drive was quiet, and it wasn't until they were almost to the museum that Grady, in the passenger seat of the Porsche, spoke. 'Nice little car,' he commented then. 'What's its top speed?'

'About a hundred and fifty. I've had it well above a hundred—on a track, of course. They get a little upset with you if you use the expressway.' Her lips were tight. 'Jeremy, hand me my sunglasses, would you? They're in the top pocket of my bag.'

Grady studied her face. 'From what Jared said, that's what Rick was doing that night—using the freeway as a racetrack.'

She didn't look at him. 'Not really. Rick always drove fast. He paid speeding tickets as nonchalantly as most people pay parking meters. It just caught up with him that night.' She braked and pulled into the parking lot. The classic columns of the Greek revival-style building gleamed in the late morning sunlight.

'I shouldn't have brought it up. I'm sorry, Elizabeth.'

She parked the car and turned in her seat to reach for her handbag. Then she met his eyes and forced a smile. 'I guess it's something I have to live with, isn't it? Just as you'll have to live with the fact that I still mourn Rick. It bothers you, doesn't it, that I forgot you so quickly?'

'You didn't have a lot of choice under the circumstances, did you, Betsy?'

'Come on,' Jeremy begged, and as soon as he was out of the car he darted up the long flight of steps to the main entrance.

Grady and Elizabeth followed more slowly, and as they started up the steps, he reached for her hand. Elizabeth let him hold it till they reached the top. Then she pulled away to fold her sunglasses and tuck them, with far more care than was necessary, back into her handbag. When he tried to recapture her hand, Elizabeth pretended not to notice. She wasn't going to let him turn this into a farce.

Four hours later she privately admitted defeat. Grady had snatched a kiss in the coal mine elevator when the guide shut off the lights momentarily to demonstrate what working conditions had been like in a real mine. And he had commented, under his breath, in the German submarine, 'Not the place for a man with claustrophobia. How would you like to try making love in one of those bunks?' Elizabeth had not thought it funny. The guide had.

She sat in the old-fashioned ice cream parlour, sipping a soda, her expression pensive as she watched her small son poring over the museum guide. He could read just enough of the words to plan where he wanted to go next.

Grady pushed his soda aside. 'There's something that really amazes me, Elizabeth,' he observed.

She looked up reluctantly. 'I suppose you want me to ask what it is?'

'It's the way you seem to feel about this child.'

'The brat?' But her tone was affectionate.

'You obviously love him very much.'

'More than you thought I could care about anyone?'

'More than I thought you would allow yourself to care,' Grady corrected.

'It's all appearances. I'm really a rotten mother, aren't I, Jeremy?'

Jeremy shook his head and pointed to an exhibit on the map. 'What does this say?'

Elizabeth read it for him and then returned to the subject. 'I don't bake cookies; I can't butter toast and get it right. . .'

Jeremy pondered the question. 'But you take me to all

the Bears games,' he pointed out logically. 'And Florence bakes cookies anyway. Can I have a dime for the nickelodeon?'

Grady fished in his pocket. 'Don't you mean a nickel?'

'Nope. It says right here.' Jeremy waved the booklet under Grady's nose.

'What happened to your allowance?' Elizabeth asked.

'I'm saving it to buy freeze-dried ice cream at the souvenir shop.' He took the dime and darted off down the turn-of-the-century Main Street.

'The awful results of inflation,' Grady mourned. 'Freeze-dried ice cream?'

'Yes. It's all the rage with his friends. Ice cream like the astronauts eat. It isn't bad, either, unless you insist on ice cream being cold.'

'I think I'll stick to the old-fashioned kind. Shall we go after the kid?' As they strolled down the cobbled street, he mused, 'It still puzzles me, that you actually took the risk of a pregnancy spoiling your figure. Not that it did, of course.' His assessing gaze summed her up, and he obviously liked what he saw. 'As a matter of fact, you're prettier now than you used to be. It's maturity, I suppose. But it makes me wonder. . .'

'Just keep wondering, Grady,' Elizabeth advised. 'It entertains me to speculate what wild explanation you'll come up with next.'

Elizabeth leaned back in the comfortable chair and closed her eyes, feeling the facial mask already tugging on her skin. It was a relief just to sit still—to know that, short of emergency, no one would bother her for the next hour. It was well worth giving up lunch for the feeling.

'What colour of polish would you like, Mrs Englin?' The manicurist held out a tray of bottles as Elizabeth opened her eyes.

She honestly couldn't have cared less, but she made a show of carefully choosing a bottle.

'That has an opalescent finish, almost like mother-of-pearl,' the girl said.

'That's fine,' Elizabeth said, and closed her eyes again. The shop was busy, but the noise receded as she relaxed into the soft upholstery and extended a hand so that the manicurist could remove the old polish.

Yes, it was worth giving up lunch, she thought again. The morning had been hectic, with several small annoyances that had built up over the weekend. The manager who had been on duty should have taken care of them. Tom would have—but then, she reminded herself, not all assistants were like Tom. He always seemed to know what she would want done and he would go ahead and do it.

The annoyances ordinarily wouldn't have been so irritating, she told herself, if the weekend hadn't been so emotionally disturbing.

But at least one of her problems had solved itself, temporarily at any rate. Corbin had left this morning, on his way to New York. It was a relief to see him go. Jeremy was right, she concluded; Corbin was becoming a bore. And despite what he had said about proposing to her, Elizabeth knew he never would. Corbin was unable—or perhaps just unwilling—to commit himself to one woman, but he expected each of the women he dated to devote herself to him alone. He was only jealous because it had been so forcefully brought to his attention that he wasn't the only man in her life. Tom he could laugh at; Corbin had never taken seriously the possibility that any woman could prefer Tom Bradford to him. But the Logan brothers were another story.

Elizabeth had had breakfast with him in the coffeeshop right before he had left for O'Hare to catch his flight. The first cup of coffee hadn't cooled before she was glad she hadn't invited him to the apartment. He had been snide and sarcastic. Elizabeth had declined to explain anything and told him to let her know in advance if he wanted her to be free on a weekend again.

Of course, she thought, a small smile cracking the facial mask, it hadn't helped Corbin's sense of humour when Grady had breezed in to apologise for missing their golf game and casually let drop that he had spent the day with Elizabeth and Jeremy. It hadn't made Elizabeth happy either. If it had been anybody but Corbin who was on the receiving end of that blow, she'd have been tempted to murder Grady right there. She was fast realising that Grady meant his threat to break up every relationship she had, no matter how casual. She supposed he'd start on Tom next.

'Oh, here's a problem. We'd better do a mending job or you'll probably lose the nail next week,' the manicurist said.

Elizabeth nodded vaguely, her mind still on Grady's threat, and on Tom. He'd apparently spent his weekend off thinking things over. When he had come into her office that morning, she had been braced for almost anything, but he had apologised for what he'd said to her about her marriage. He wouldn't listen when Elizabeth had also tried to apologise. Instead he'd invited her to have dinner with him the next evening. She had tried to beg off, since she had decided not to go out with him again. But he'd reminded her gently that it was his birthday, and she had finally agreed. She sighed. She should have been more careful not to let him get serious about her. Now, she supposed, he would be looking for another job, and she would lose the best assistant manager she had ever had, as well as a good friend. Myles had been right; socialising with employees was a bad idea.

The repair made to the damaged nail, the manicurist began applying the first coat of the opalescent polish.

Elizabeth put her head back and closed her eyes again. She began marshalling the facts that she would need to have at her fingertips in the interview this afternoon. The reporter would be arriving in another hour. She hoped the man wouldn't be too persistent with his questions; she wasn't up to holding off a siege. Perhaps if she could anticipate some of the questions it would be easier.

When she stirred a few minutes later, the second coat of polish was already on her nails. Elizabeth looked at them and shook her head, hardly believing that she could have gone off to sleep in the middle of a manicure. But the cosmetologist was coming back to remove her facial mask.

The white-haired woman in the next chair chuckled. 'You've been doing too much sightseeing,' she advised. 'Do you feel better now that you've had a nap?'

'A little,' Elizabeth admitted. The girl cracked the mask with a warm towel and started to take it off.

'I always make it a point to get my hair fixed every day when I'm travelling,' the woman added. Her voice was muffled by the mask on her face. When the towels came off Elizabeth's face, she realised that all she could see of the woman was enormous blue eyes. 'My husband thinks it's a terrible waste of time—but then I think his business meetings are,' she drawled.

'That's not very flattering of him.' Elizabeth lay back, and the cosmetologist reached for her foundation cream.

The woman chuckled. 'At my age, it's true. But it relaxes me to have someone fussing over me.'

A voice came from the chair on Elizabeth's left. 'It is an agreeable luxury, isn't it?'

Elizabeth didn't turn. She wanted to groan. Of all the ways to ruin a lunchtime facial, finding Anne Andrews in the next chair had to be the all-time winner. The girl must have come in while she had been dozing. 'Hi, Anne,' she said, forcing herself to be cordial. 'I didn't expect to see you here.'

'Oh, my regular girl is on vacation, so I thought I'd see how good this shop is. I was in the neighbourhood.'

I'll bet, Elizabeth thought. Just hoping to be in the lobby when Grady comes home for lunch, is more like it.

Anne added, 'I tried to get Mother to come with me, but she was much too busy with all of the preparations for the débutante ball. So many things have to be done right now. And of course, she never misses an appointment with her regular salon and she hates to break her schedule. I'm so fortunate, I know, to have inherited her complexion; I never have a speck of trouble. I should have thought you—but then you are quite a bit older than I, aren't you, Elizabeth? Ten years or so?'

There was a stifled gasp from the cosmetologist.

Elizabeth smiled tightly. She had wondered how long it would be before Anne brought the conflict out into the open. It wasn't surprising that she was on the offensive after she had been dismissed like a child on the balcony on Saturday night. But that hadn't been Elizabeth's doing. She wondered idly what the girl would do if she said, 'Anne, you're welcome to the big lug. Just keep him out of my way.' She toyed with the idea a moment, then said, 'I wouldn't have phrased our age difference quite that way, Anne. I'd have said you're a mere baby. Don't be in too great a hurry to join the big leagues.'

Anne shrugged. 'I long ago stopped worrying about people who think I'm too young to do what I want. And as far as age goes, you couldn't have been much older than I when that little boy of yours was born—were you? And I'd say that's getting into the big leagues.'

Elizabeth closed her eyes so the cosmetologist could apply shadow. 'I was twenty,' she mused.

'Only a year older. And if I may say so, a lot of people probably think I'm choosing much more wisely than you did. After all, you were divorced before the baby was even born!'

Elizabeth counted to ten and said softly, 'I wouldn't forget, if I were you, Anne, that it isn't only you who will do the choosing. I imagine Grady will have something to say about it.'

Anne sniffled. 'Whoever put those green eyes into your head certainly knew what your nature would be, Elizabeth. You're a jealous and catty woman. Well, you can just give up any ideas you have of getting in my way. You don't really think a Logan would settle for a divorced woman with a child, do you? Don't be naïve. Grady and Jared Logan can look as high as they like when they choose their wives. There was even a rumour about Grady and a princess, over in Europe.'

Elizabeth let the silence lengthen as she inspected her make-up in the mirror. She knew that anything she said would go straight to Vicki, and if she said too much, the débutante ball might be held at the Palmer House this year. She wished Tonya were here—Tonya had never in her life let anyone run over her. And come to think of it, why should Elizabeth run scared of a teenager? Vicki was a social leader, but so was Elizabeth. And if the ball wasn't held at the Englin, it wouldn't be the end of the world.

She dabbed a bit more eyeshadow on and tipped her lashes more heavily with mascara. She smiled at the cosmetologist, slipped a note into the girl's hand, and stood up. 'I should think Grady's reputation would give you qualms, Anne,' she said softly. 'If he's been sleeping with a princess, whatever makes you think he'll marry a teenager who hasn't learned to stop giggling and playing silly games?'

CHAPTER SEVEN

'Turn your head just a little more to the left,' the photographer requested, and moved a floodlight a few inches.

Elizabeth obediently turned her head and stifled a sigh. She knew how important it was to co-operate with the Press, but this session was getting out of hand. She shifted her weight and leaned a little more against the ornate railing of the grand staircase in the main lobby. It seemed she'd been standing here for hours. Think positive, Elizabeth, she told herself. At least all of the questions were behind her.

The photographer looked up. 'I like that pose,' he said. 'Hold it right there!' He clicked the shutter. Elizabeth stood up straight, and the photographer cried, 'No! Just a couple more, please, Mrs Englin.'

Though it was phrased as a request, it was more of an order. Elizabeth sighed and said, 'How long is this going to go on? I set aside two hours for this interview; it's taken almost three now.'

The reporter came slowly up the staircase. 'Just a few more minutes, Mrs Englin,' he said. His voice oozed charm. 'You wouldn't want just any old picture on the news-stand, would you?' He smoothed the shoulder of her dress. 'Just be patient.'

'I'd watch where I put my hands if I were you,' a voice recommended lazily from the top of the staircase. 'Even if Elizabeth is too polite to push you down the stairs, I'm not.' Grady, in dinner clothes, came down to stand beside her. 'Now, I believe you said—one more picture?'

'But. . .'

'I get very impatient when I have a dinner date and

someone is delaying my companion,' Grady mused.

The reporter looked at him sourly. 'Right, Mr Logan. One more picture.'

The photograph was taken, and the equipment was packed away. When the revolving doors had ushered the newsmen on to the street, Elizabeth said, 'Sometimes I have to admit that your aggressiveness does come in handy. But I don't have a dinner date with you.'

'Yes, you do. You didn't deny it a few minutes ago; therefore, you agreed to it. And it would be such a shame to waste that lovely dress. You should always wear green, you know. It's by far your best colour.' He picked up the hem of the chiffon sleeve, cut wide to fall like a cape, let it drift down around her wrist, and took her arm. 'Very nice,' he said. 'Where would you like to go?'

'I promised Myles I'd be at home tonight.'

'He thinks it's pretty strange that you don't ever want to have anything to do with me. He just can't imagine what you have against me.'

'Maybe I should tell him,' Elizabeth threatened.

'Darling, you know that would tempt me to retaliate. And you know who would come off best in that exchange. Look at it this way—if you ever hope to convince him that you won't consider me as a husband, you'll have to give me a fair chance.'

They reached the elevator lobby. 'Why don't you just name your wedding-day? That would be all the convincing Myles needs. I'm positive Annie won't hold out for a long engagement.'

'Her name is Anne.'

'Sorry. I keep forgetting that she's no longer a child. Quite.'

He smiled at that. 'You think I'm robbing the cradle, don't you?'

'Yes. You do realise that you can't even buy her a drink anywhere in the state of Illinois? You'd be supplying alcohol to a minor. But I'm sure the age difference has some advantages. You can bring her up according to your own rules, this way. It should prevent quite a lot of arguments.'

'Whereas you and I would fight all the time,' he agreed.

'Probably. Independence gets to be a habit, you know.'

'I'd say in your case you were born independent. Rick must have had quite a time keeping you under control'.

'He never tried.' The elevator stopped on Elizabeth's floor.

'I don't imagine any of your men ever had much luck at that. It would be interesting to see how you'd behave if someone actually did it. You're a bit like dynamite, you know. Safe as a rock when properly handled. But if the wrong person gets hold of it. . .' He followed her into the hall.

'Grady—remember? You live one floor up,' Elizabeth reminded, pointing at the ceiling.

'Yes, I know. I'm coming to dinner.'

'I didn't invite you.'

'Luckily, Myles did. I told him we'd be straight up unless I could persuade you to go out.' He held out a hand for her door key.

Elizabeth sighed and handed it over. 'I have never met a more domineering, opinionated. . .'

'Wait till you know Jared better. He's the all-time champion.' He guided her into the drawing room. 'It didn't take much to get her away from work, Myles. Just a threat to punch a reporter in the nose.'

'And now they'll probably make me look like a hag,' Elizabeth complained.

'Stop fishing for compliments,' Grady ordered and handed her a Manhattan. 'You can trust the company tonight,' he said softly.

'I'm not so sure,' Elizabeth replied, but she took the drink.

'Aren't Whit and Mother here yet?' Grady asked.

'Jeremy's showing them the view from the terrace. Would you give me a refill, my boy?' Myles handed Grady his ginger-ale glass.

'Whit and whom?' Elizabeth asked. She set her Manhattan down on the coffee table with a hand that shook slightly. All she needed now was Jared and her day would be complete.

'My mother. Here comes Jeremy,' Grady announced.

Jeremy flung his arms around Elizabeth. 'I thought you were home.'

'How could you know? I just got here.'

He shrugged. 'I always know. I played with John today, and I went with Florence to the market. . .'

Elizabeth listened patiently to the childish prattle. She had missed so many hours of her son's growing up that the ones she could spend with him were precious.

He curled up on the couch next to her and snuggled his head into her shoulder. 'Are we going to buy my school clothes this week? It's only a few days till school starts.'

'It's still more than two weeks, honey. But we'll go Friday morning. And if you're patient about trying everything on, we'll do something special.'

She looked up and caught Grady watching her thoughtfully. She flushed a little and held her chin higher. She supposed he was still pondering why she had risked spoiling a near-perfect figure to have a baby. She was an unorthodox mother, she knew—so much so that some of her friends thought Jeremy was deprived. But this aching love for him was nothing to be ashamed of. If that puzzled Grady, it certainly wasn't her problem.

Myles said, 'Helene, I'd like to present my granddaughter Elizabeth.'

Elizabeth hadn't seen the couple come in from the terrace. Automatically she started to nudge Jeremy's head from her shoulder so she could rise. But a warm drawl said, 'Oh, don't get up, my dear. You both look so

comfortable, and I'm charmed to see a child so affectionate towards his mother.'

Elizabeth looked up, green eyes wide with shock. 'Oh,
no. . .' she whispered.

The lady from the beauty shop chuckled. 'I'm sorry I
didn't introduce myself earlier, but I didn't want to be
responsible for the damage when your—friend—sank
through the floor. I'm fairly certain she would have if
she'd known who I was.' She sat down next to Jeremy.

'I'm mortified,' Elizabeth said. 'I could sink through
the floor now—all twenty-three of them.'

'Oh, come now. It was the funniest thing I've heard in
months, and you certainly came off the winner. It took her
ten minutes to recuperate after you left, and even then she
was only muttering incoherently.'

'Mrs Logan, I am so ashamed. I shouldn't have been
practising on Anne—she is only a child, after all, and. . .'

'My name is Helene. And don't fuss about it so, dear. If
you hadn't said it, I'd have been tempted, and that would
have been unforgivable. It's quite true, you know. I don't
know what Grady's thinking of—a teenager!' She sipped
her drink, her blue eyes studying Elizabeth's face. 'And
what a teenager, though I don't think I'd call her a child.'

Elizabeth refused to be drawn.

Helene set her glass down. 'If you don't smile, I'm
going to have this child tickle you,' she said. 'Whit and
Myles are looking over here, wondering what on earth
we've managed to quarrel about already. Now smile! I
should think you'd need a sense of humour, Elizabeth.'

Elizabeth smiled at that. 'It's taken a beating in the last
week,' she admitted.

'That's better. Life is much easier if you can laugh
about things—believe me, I know. Living with Whit for
thirty-five years has taught me that.'

Elizabeth privately thought that living with Whit
Logan for six months would have soured the average

woman on living at all, or left her with no personality of her own, but Helene was an unusual person. Apparently, part of her success was because she remained in the background. Elizabeth couldn't remember Myles saying much about Helene, and while Grady had told her quite a bit about his father, his mother had been mentioned only in passing.

Elizabeth sipped her drink. 'All of the men in your family are a little overwhelming, aren't they?'

'How did you notice?' Helene asked dryly. 'I keep hoping that in subsequent generations it will be diluted—but so far, I've had no luck in finding out what will happen. Our boys seem to be even more intense than Whit. Who knows what their children will be like? Of course, if Grady actually marries this young miss. . .'

Elizabeth looked down into her glass, swirled the ice cubes, and set it down. 'Did you come especially to visit Grady, or are you travelling through?'

Helene's eyes sparkled, 'I see you don't want to talk about Anne. Very well, we won't. We've been on a Pacific cruise for two weeks, and we're just on our way home.'

'It must have been lovely.'

'The first week was beautiful. We cruised up to Alaska, and the scenery is magnificent. The last few days Whit has been impatient to get home. I think he would have jumped ship a week ago if he hadn't been fifty miles offshore.'

Elizabeth laughed. 'I'm surprised he didn't call for a helicopter to rescue him.'

Whit chuckled. 'I would have if I'd thought of it. Next time I'll take you along, Elizabeth. Grady, as long as you're tending bar. . .'

'I may just give up banking and go into the night-club business,' Grady mused. He picked up Elizabeth's glass. 'Another Manhattan?'

'No, thanks, I'm still sipping this one.'

'What a spoil-sport. Come on, Jeremy, you can carry

the drinks back. You can't expect a good bartender to be a waiter, too.'

Jeremy slid off the couch. 'Can I have a glass of wine?' he asked with a mischievous look at Elizabeth.

'Jeremy,' she protested. 'I know I'm a rotten parent, but you don't have to rub it in.'

'Some ginger-ale, then?' Jeremy sighed.

Helene watched the child as Grady poured his ginger-ale. 'He's a sweet child, Elizabeth,' she commented. 'He's so friendly, and very charming.'

'Oh, when he makes up his mind to it, he can charm your socks off without disturbing your shoes.'

'Yes, I can imagine that,' Helene mused. 'He's like you in colouring, of course.'

'Yes.' Elizabeth took another nervous sip from her glass and watched as Jeremy crossed the room to perch on a stool beside Whit's chair. The grey-haired man smiled down at the child and let his hand rest casually on Jeremy's shoulder as he talked to Myles. With determination, Elizabeth turned back to Helene and said cheerfully, 'The staff here spoil him dreadfully, you know. When he's crossed he can be a real torment. Will you be staying long?'

'No, we leave tomorrow for New York. We just wanted to see Grady's new home, and since Jared happened to be here, too, it seemed too good a chance to miss. They're so seldom in the same state any more.'

'Where is Jared tonight?'

'He's with a client. They didn't expect us for another day or two. By the way, Grady's apartment is beautiful. Myles said you do all of the decorating for the hotel?'

Grady crossed the room with a fresh drink and sat down on the arm of the couch beside Elizabeth.

She shifted uneasily away from him and said, 'For the penthouses and suites, yes. It's my one domestic talent. My culinary expertise extends to taking the croissants out of the bakery box; I once tried to sew an apron and ended up with a potholder; and when a green plant sees me coming it commits suicide. But I can redecorate a room.'

'She can't cook, either,' Jeremy announced, and looked surprised when everyone laughed.

Grady leaned an elbow on the back of the couch just behind her head and told his mother, 'Don't believe a word of it. Elizabeth has many domestic talents.'

'Like what?' she retorted, and was instantly sorry, for Grady's smile promised that she wouldn't like his answer.

Across the room, Whit chuckled. 'You'd better watch out for him, Elizabeth,' he said lazily. 'A lot of people have made the mistake of underestimating Grady. They don't generally do it twice.' He looked at his son with an approving smile.

Elizabeth was irritated. It was just the sort of thing Whit would have been proud of, she reflected. Anything that increased the profitability of the Logan banks, regardless of its effects on people, would be approved. The more cold-blooded the better.

Whit went on, 'Are you still converting all of your suites into apartments?'

'Yes. In fact, the Carlisle was rented today,' she told Myles. 'As soon as the decorators are finished, the new tenants will move in.'

'It will be nice to have company up there,' Grady murmured. 'Especially if she's nice-looking?' It was a question.

'She's remarkable.' Elizabeth drained her glass and set it aside. 'For sixty-five and holding.'

He shrugged. 'Surely somebody in Chicago has both good looks and the money to afford a penthouse at the Englin.'

'Most of them with that combination head for Hollywood. Or the Bahamas.' She was remembering what

Grady had said about her being the type to lounge in the sun on a Caribbean island.

'You didn't,' Whit observed.

'But then that's hardly the same thing, is it, Whit?' Grady asked idly.

Elizabeth's cheeks flamed. She turned to stare at him, hoping to convince him to be quiet. What Whit already knew about her was too much.

Grady merely smiled. 'She doesn't look like the kind who could manage so much as a chequebook, does she?'

'Sexist,' she muttered under her breath.

'Lucky for you that Elizabeth was able to take over so much of the responsibility when you had to give it up, Myles,' Whit said. 'Both of us have been fortunate, you know—that the younger members of the family want to follow in the business.'

Grady made a sound that Elizabeth would have uncharitably described as a snort. Only she heard it.

Whit continued, 'And what was that you were saying about domestic talents, Grady?'

Grady looked down at Elizabeth and started to answer. Elizabeth held her breath. But just then Florence announced dinner.

'You were saved by the bell, literally, you know,' Grady murmured, as he extended a hand to help her up.

'You can just be quiet about it, too. My attributes are none of your business,' Elizabeth threatened.

Grady was the picture of outraged innocence. 'Darling, I don't say anything I don't mean. And if you've forgotten which domestic talents I was talking about, I'll just take you out on the terrace after dinner, and we'll look at the moon, and I'll remind you.'

Elizabeth stopped at the open door of Tom's office. 'Happy birthday,' she called.

He looked up from the calculator on his desk. 'Hi,

Elizabeth. I've been meaning to ask you—don't you think all employees should get their birthdays off? A paid holiday, of course.'

'If we put that in the staff handbook, you'd be amazed to find that fully half the staff was born on Christmas Day,' she said. 'Just so they're certain never to have to work it again. That's a pretty plant. It's new, isn't it?' She leaned over the desk to caress a fuzzy, purple-veined leaf on the plant, which cascaded over the corner of the desk from a dark brown ceramic pot.

'Yes—a birthday gift from Jill.' He sounded preoccupied.

'Our new assistant? I'll bet she grew it herself. Maybe she even made the pot. I told you she was domestic, Thomas.'

'I remember.' He didn't sound interested. 'Our dinner reservation is for eight tonight. At the Gentleman's Club. Is that all right?'

'Fine. I love that place—all the old leather and soft lighting. Just like London in the 1890s.'

'Shall I come up for you?'

'No, I'll meet you here in the office.' There was no point in letting Myles have the opportunity to say anything about it. Elizabeth wouldn't lie to him about dating Tom, but she saw no reason to call it to his attention, either. She was thinking about that as she went on down the hall to her own office. She had spent a great deal of her life, it seemed, in making sure that Myles continued to be happily ignorant. Perhaps it would have been better to have always told the truth, she thought.

Her secretary put the telephone down and asked, 'How is the work going on the Carlisle?'

'Slow, but the contractor promised to be finished by Labor Day. Would you call the tenants and tell them they can move in by the tenth of the month? That should give us enough time for the finishing touches.' She had picked up the sheaf of messages as she spoke and was flipping through them. Alan McConnell needed to talk to her about a lawsuit filed by a hotel guest who had slipped in a bathtub. Grady Logan had called to say good morning and to ask if she'd enjoyed her morning newspaper. 'What does this mean?' Elizabeth asked.

The secretary shrugged. 'That's all he said—did she enjoy her morning paper.'

Elizabeth scowled, wadded the scrap of paper up, and threw it as hard as she could at the nearest wastebasket. Then she went back to her message slips. Her accountant wanted to fix a date for the next audit. And Vicki Andrews regretted that she would be unable to keep their luncheon date.

'Nice of her to give me notice,' Elizabeth said cynically, glancing at the clock. It was half past twelve; Tonya would be arriving any minute; their table was booked for one o'clock.

The secretary looked sympathetic. 'She was very cold about it.' Curiosity gleamed in her eyes.

Elizabeth shrugged it off. Obviously Anne had reported their conversation yesterday to Vicki. There goes the débutante ball, she thought philosophically. Well, it wasn't worth having if she had to sit still for being insulted by a teenager. Though she almost wished that Helene had introduced herself yesterday in the salon. It would have been well worth seeing the expression on Anne's face when she found herself confronted by the woman she hoped would be her mother-in-law.

'Am I late?' Tonya breezed into the office and looked around. 'Well, if I've beaten Vicki here, I must be ahead of schedule.'

'She isn't coming. Which probably means she's on the phone with another hotel in the Loop making arrangements for the débutante ball.'

'It didn't sit too well with her, I take it?'

Elizabeth was startled. 'How did you know about it?'

'Darling, everybody in Chicago knows about it.'

There was silence for an instant. Then Elizabeth said, 'Are we talking about the same thing?'

'I assumed we were. Why do you think Vicki's mad, anyway?'

'Because I got catty with Anne yesterday. But nobody could know that!'

'No, but I'd love to hear about it,' Tonya's expression was rapt. 'Do you mean to tell me you don't know about the newspaper item? You really don't? Come on.' She seized Elizabeth's arm and almost dragged her out of the office and down the mezzanine steps to the main lobby.

'What newspaper item?' Elizabeth asked with foreboding. 'Is that what that message was about?'

'What message?' Tonya bought a copy of the morning paper at the information desk and started down the hall towards the Captain's Table restaurant. 'I assume we're eating here?'

'Yes. Tell me about the newspaper item!' Elizabeth begged.

'Here. Read it yourself.' Tonya shook out a section of the newspaper and folded it back. 'Now, is that you, or isn't it?'

Elizabeth took the paper and glanced down the gossip column to the item at the end. 'The loveliest lady hotelkeeper in the Windy City is being squired by one of the nation's wealthiest young bankers, who has, of late, become very possessive of the lady's time. Will it be wedding bells? or something less formal?'

Elizabeth could have screamed.

She stared, stunned, at the newspaper. It was one of the most widely read columns in the city; Myles had certainly seen it by now. And of all the days for it to appear, it had to be when Whit and Helene were in town. They would have heard about it sooner or later, anyway; she wasn't sure if the column was syndicated, but some well-meaning friend would have been certain to call it to their attention. But for this to appear in the papers on the one day of the year when they were under the same roof—! They deserved a better reception than this. She put a hand to the back of her neck. It didn't surprise her that she suddenly had the world's champion of headaches.

And Grady seemed to think the whole thing was funny! Elizabeth wished that, for once in her life, she could stop wondering what everyone was thinking about her. But she had lived under the shadow of gossip for so long that she couldn't just laugh it off. Her guilty memories found hidden meaning in every comment that was made about her.

'Now do you know why Vicki couldn't make it to lunch?' Tonya turned to the maitre d'. 'Two, please, in Mrs Englin's name.'

Elizabeth sank into a chair at the back of the restaurant and wanted to crawl into the newspaper and disappear. Half a dozen patrons had recognised her and waved, but the smiles that a few minutes ago would have been friendly now looked, to her guilty eyes, malicious.

'I'll kill him for doing this to me,' she said.

'Who?' Tonya asked practically. 'Grady or the reporter who wrote it?'

'Both of them.'

Tonya shrugged. 'The reporter was just doing his job. And Grady's only having a bit of fun, at your expense.'

'Grady's definition of a bit of fun makes the Marquis de Sade look like a spinster schoolteacher.' Elizabeth's teeth were clenched.

'Oh, come on. Vicki will come down off her high ropes as soon as the gossip dies away. Which it will do a lot faster if you don't get all excited about it. What looks good to eat?'

'Absolutely nothing,' Elizabeth said bitterly. 'And I

don't give a damn about the débutante ball. I just don't want my name linked with his anywhere, much less in the daily papers.'

Tonya laid the menu aside. Concern was suddenly uppermost in her mind. 'You are really upset, aren't you, Elizabeth?'

'How did you ever guess?'

'Do you know what I'd do?'

'No, but I'm sure you'll tell me.'

'I'd go up to Lord and Taylor's this afternoon and make a production out of looking at wedding gowns. Play up to it, Elizabeth—make a joke out of it. That way Vicki will be the one who ends up looking like a fool.'

'Thanks for saying I'm a fool, Tonya.'

'That wasn't what I said. I'll have the broccoli quiche,' she told the waitress, and took the unused menu out of Elizabeth's hand.

'Make it two,' Elizabeth murmured.

'You could even joke about needing a gown with an expandable waistline. . .'

'That is not funny.'

'All right, but don't get so absolutely livid, Elizabeth. It will just convince everybody that you're trying to hid something. And then Grady would really have fun.'

'Not to mention all the other people who consider themselves my friends.'

'Right. Even Alan picked up on it right away. He asked me after the dance Saturday what was going on.'

'I can't imagine what tipped him off.'

'Sarcasm doesn't suit you.' Tonya pushed the sugar across the table. 'Come, now, put the sugar in your coffee like a good girl, and take a sip, and smile at me so all the busybodies who are watching you will be convinced everything is normal.'

Elizabeth did. 'Why do I feel like you're talking to Brian?'

'Because you're acting like Brian does. That's better. Now let's gossip about somebody else. Is Grady really going to marry Anne?'

'I love how you change the subject, Tonya. He won't if his mother has anything to say about it—but then, of course, Anne's mother is in favour, so that balances out. It'll probably depend on how much of her father's bank she'll inherit. If marriage comes out cheaper than a merger, he'll marry her.'

'Elizabeth, you're turning into a green-eyed Persian cat.'

'I'm not a Persian, but I'll admit that the rest of that is true. Whenever that girl comes near me, I put out my claws.'

'It happens to the best of us. If you don't want to shop for wedding gowns. . .'

'I don't. And I wouldn't shop at Lord and Taylor for one, anyway. I'd wear my grandmother's dress—if I ever need such a thing.'

'That's my girl. I think you should say that a little louder, actually. Let's go up to Tiffany's then, so I can pick out what Alan's buying me for our anniversary.'

'Do you always buy your own gifts?'

'Always. He has terrible taste in jewellery.'

The waitress set their plates down. 'What is this?' Elizabeth asked, poking at it with her fork.

'Broccoli quiche.'

'That's what I was afraid of. I hate broccoli.'

'Then why did you order it?' Tonya picked up her fork. 'Now tell me all about Anne and whatever it was that happened yesterday.'

CHAPTER EIGHT

TOM took the last bite of his steak and watched Elizabeth toy with her veal Parmesan. 'If you don't start eating better, I'm going to quit taking you out,' he teased.

Elizabeth forced a smile. 'Sorry, Tom. I just don't feel that I should be here.'

'Why not? It's my birthday, and I want to spend it with you. I want to spend all my birthdays with you.' He lit a cigarette and inhaled deeply. 'And all my Christmases . . . and Valentine's Days. . .'

She shook her head sadly.

'What is it, Elizabeth? What have I done? A couple of weeks ago, I thought you agreed with me that we might be able to live our lives together. What's changed?'

'You haven't done anything, Tom. I've changed, I guess. It was a mistake for us to start dating.'

He swirled the wine in his glass thoughtfully. 'Is it Logan?' he asked abruptly. He drained the glass and reached for the carafe.

'Why do you ask that?' Elizabeth asked cautiously.

He looked up at her, the light slanting across his face and highlighting the cheekbones, and drew deeply on the cigarette. 'I know it isn't Corbin Evans,' he said. 'You've been seeing him for a couple of years, and he's obviously not important to you. Then Grady Logan comes to town, and overnight you're a different person. And everywhere one of you is, there's the other one too.' He stubbed the cigarette out viciously.

'That's hardly been my choice,' Elizabeth said dryly. She sipped her wine and looked up at the low-beamed ceiling. The Gentleman's Club was her favourite place to eat, and Tom knew it. It might not be such a favourite after this evening, she realised. It looked as if Tom might be difficult tonight.

'You could have stopped it. You never had any trouble with unwanted attentions before.'

'That wasn't Grady.' Her tone was thoughtful. It was true; even while she was a co-ed she'd had a way of convincing men that she was untouchable. Some of her sorority sisters had snippily referred to her as the Ice Maiden because of it. But Grady had never taken no for an answer. From their first meeting, it was as though her shield just didn't work when he was around. All he had to do was show up, and she fell apart.

'Then it is him who's caused the change.'

'Why does it have to be anybody?'

'I just mean that something has changed you. The only variable I can think of is Logan. I wish I understood why.' He refilled her wineglass. 'Are you going to marry him?'

'You've been reading the gossip columns.' Elizabeth's voice was steady. Not bad, she congratulated herself. It was considerably calmer than when she'd been with Tonya when she had handed her the paper at lunch. They had spent the afternoon trying on clothes in all of the exclusive shops at Water Tower Place—a pastime guaranteed to raise the spirits of any woman. Not that it had returned her to normal, but her veneer was back in place.

'I didn't see it myself, I'll admit. Jill pointed it out to me,' Tom said.

And you will probably never forgive her for doing it, Elizabeth thought. Just as I will never forgive Grady for landing me in this situation, with everyone in Chicago laughing at me behind my back, all over again.

'Elizabeth?'

'I'm sorry. I was just thinking about that ridiculous

item.' If she kept telling herself it was only ridiculous, perhaps she'd come to believe it.

Tom shrugged. 'From where I stand, it looks very believable.' He pulled out another cigarette and flicked his lighter, holding her gaze over the steady flame.

'It's nothing but a piece of gossip, Tom. But that nosy reporter of yours certainly didn't lose any time selling a choice titbit.'

'He's not my nosy reporter.'

'I just wish that when you warned me to be careful what I said to him, you'd have warned Grady too. That stupid reporter and his photographer were taking so fearfully long, and I couldn't get rid of them. They had me posing on the grand staircase—you were right about that, by the way, evening gown and all—and Grady told the guy to keep his hands off me or he'd push him down the stairs. Then he let them have one more picture, and kicked them out.'

'Boy,' Tom said sarcastically, 'I don't see where the reporter made a little thing like that into being possessive. My God, if I tried to step into something like that, you'd have pushed *me* down the stairs!'

'If I hadn't been so tired of the photographs, I just might have done that.'

Tom's look was unbelieving. After a moment, he said, 'You didn't answer my question. Are you going to marry him?'

'Let me put it this way, Tom—there are at least two other people in this city as irritated as I am about that gossip column. One of them is Grady's unofficial fiancée and the other one is her mother.'

'Not Logan?'

'Oh, no. He considers it a prime joke, at least judging by the messages he's leaving for me.'

The waiter cleared their places. 'Are you ready for dessert, sir?' he asked. 'And perhaps a light wine?'

Tom nodded. Then, suddenly, he tensed in his chair. 'Speak of the devil,' he said.

'Who? Grady? It doesn't surprise me.'

'I said just a minute ago, where one of you is, the other is sure to be.'

'Believe me, I didn't invite him,' Elizabeth said tartly. 'The man has a gift—or a curse, from my point of view. Nobody ever tells him where I am, or at least no one will ever admit to telling him. He just knows.'

The waiter returned with a small double-layered cake with a single candle on it. 'From the lady,' he said, placing it in front of Tom with a flourish.

'Happy birthday, Tom,' Elizabeth said, and reached into her handbag for a small square package, gaily wrapped in silver paper.

'I wonder if I have enough breath to blow out the candle,' Tom wondered.

'Don't forget to make your wish, sir,' the waiter said with a smile, and poured their coffee.

Tom's eyes met Elizabeth's, and she could see the gleam of hope in their depths. Then he closed his eyes for an instant and blew out the candle.

Elizabeth sampled the cake and laid her fork down to watch Tom open his package. When he pulled out the gold money clip with his initials engraved on it, he smiled and said, 'Thank you, Elizabeth. I'd been wanting a status symbol, and you've hit on just the right one.' He took a bite of the cake. 'Watch out—here comes trouble.'

'Who is he with?'

'Dark hair, red dress. Young.'

'Anne. That should soothe her mother's rumpled feathers.'

Anne fluttered up to their table. 'Elizabeth, it's so nice to see you. I just had to come over to the table; we didn't see you when we came in, and I didn't want you to think I was cutting you.' Her eyes were cold, despite the smile.

You certainly didn't want to take a chance, Elizabeth thought. Not with Grady around to see. I could hurt you if I tried hard enough, even if your mother is a social leader. And you're not so sure that I couldn't take him away from you if I tried hard enough. You silly child, can't you believe that I don't care?

But she smiled and said, 'Heavens, Anne, that wasn't necessary. It's so crowded in here, it would be quite possible to miss half a dozen acquaintances. I certainly wouldn't have misinterpreted your motives. Hello, Grady.' Suddenly she was very conscious of the plunge neckline of her pistachio-coloured dress.

'Hi, Elizabeth. Your birthday? No, yours is in December, isn't it? You're a Sagittarius—independent, adventurous, not easily pinned down. . .'

'You've been doing your research, haven't you? Have Whit and Helene left?' Elizabeth asked. 'We enjoyed the evening with them.' She heard Anne's faint intake of breath and smiled inwardly. It was fun to rub it in a little. No doubt Grady would have to defend himself as soon as they were back at their own table, for not introducing Anne to his parents. Elizabeth only hoped that she could be there for that meeting.

'Yes, they got a noon flight from O'Hare. It was fun last night, wasn't it? We'll have to do it again. Mother was very taken by you.'

Elizabeth wondered for an instant if he had meant to say, taken in by you. But she dismissed the thought. 'That's what I was afraid of,' she muttered.

Grady flashed a smile and said, 'Happy birthday, Bradford.'

'Thank you.' Tom's voice was stiff. He shook another cigarette out of the pack and reached for his lighter. Elizabeth picked up a pack of matches, snapped one into flame, and held it to the tip of his cigarette. It was an intimate, wifely action, and it took Tom off guard.

It hadn't escaped Grady's eyes either. He smiled and said softly, 'You were always subtle, Betsy. Frequently you didn't expect others to be—but you always were.'

She shrugged. If she was subtle, it was more than he was. Grady had never been subtle in his life; if there was something there that he wanted, he announced it and went after it. She'd never forget the day he had told her he intended to make love to her. She had laughed at him, but less than a day later she was in bed with him. Then it was his turn to laugh at her, for his touch could set her afire and make her forget that she had never intended to fall in love. It still astonished her five years later, when she remembered those velvet days, that she, who chose her friends slowly and for life, had allowed Grady to make love to her on less than two days' acquaintance.

'You're blushing, Betsy,' Grady told her softly. 'Are you remembering the good old days?'

'The old days were not particularly good,' she said icily.

He smiled, but let her remark pass. 'Did you get the going-over this morning, too?'

'It was reverse psychology this time.' Myles had been very diplomatic about it at the breakfast table, his only apparent concern her future happiness. Still, he had managed to make very plain that he'd been shocked by Grady's behaviour and lack of respect for Elizabeth, and that he was now questioning how compatible they would be. He'd even apologised for trying to push them at each other. All of which, Elizabeth was sure, was exactly the opposite of what he really felt. After all, nothing had changed since yesterday. He hadn't even seen the gossip columns when he had had the little talk with her.

'That must be my mother's touch.' Grady's voice was thoughtful.

'I expect so. Myles usually comes straight out with what he thinks. That's why he wasn't very convincing this morning.'

'I haven't the faintest idea what you two are talking about,' Anne announced.

Grady just smiled. 'Never mind, Anne, it's just a new game we're playing. In any case, our waiter is hovering, and we'd better let these two get on with their celebration.'

After they were gone, Tom and Elizabeth lingered over their coffee. Tom's eyes kept shifting towards the area of the room where the other couple sat.

Elizabeth finally said, 'Is there something in the south-east corner of this restaurant that fascinates you?'

Tom flushed. 'No,' he said, stirring his coffee. 'Not really. Do you mean to tell me that he prefers her to you?'

'She's the unofficial fiancée, yes.'

Tom shook his head. 'He's crazy.'

Elizabeth laughed, 'Tom, you've restored my sense of self-worth. Thank you!'

He reached for her hand. 'Elizabeth, is my wish going to come true? Will you marry me?'

Elizabeth sobered. 'No, Tom. I'm sorry.'

He sighed. 'Then I won't bring it up again. I guess I know when it's final. Let's go.'

The apartment was quiet when she let herself in. She sighed in relief at not having to explain to Myles why she was home so early. She hadn't invited Tom to come upstairs; she just couldn't face it if he brought the subject up again, and despite what he'd said, she didn't think he really accepted that she meant it. He looked so much like a hurt puppy that she couldn't bear it. And yet she didn't see where she could have done anything differently. Tom had been right about one thing; two weeks ago she had thought she might eventually marry him. And why not? He was a nice guy; he was utterly reliable; he liked Jeremy—what a catalogue of virtues for a prospective husband, she told herself cynically. Never a word about love.

When she looked into Jeremy's room, he was sound asleep, fair hair tousled, long dark lashes lying heavily across his flushed cheeks, his pyjamas rumpled. She sat down in the rocker and watched him sleep, remembering how she had lain awake at night and watched his father sleep—as if something deep inside had told her how short their time together was to be. She drew a deep breath and banished the thought. There was no use dwelling in a past that was forever gone. That was a dream long ago shattered. Her problem now was—where was she going from here?

If Grady's coming had done nothing else, it had shown her that her life was a stagnant backwater. She had a responsible job, she had a child to watch out for, but nothing else really touched her any more. She had hundreds of acquaintances—but few friends. She had many dates—but no one man with whom she felt free to talk about the most important part of her life. She had walled that part of her from the rest of the world. Even Tom, close as he had been to her, had no real idea of what lay behind Elizabeth's cool façade, constructed painstakingly, layer by layer, through five years. But let Grady Logan walk into the room and that façade cracked. She laughed at herself, wryly. And underneath that front, what was left? Not even she was sure. She'd told him once that Betsy Ames was gone. She hadn't known how right she had been.

Jeremy stirred and flung an arm up over his head. She tucked the sheet up around him and dropped a kiss on his cheek. He opened his eyes and smiled sleepily. 'G'night, Mommy,' he murmured. She was touched. In the light of day she was 'Mom' and he frequently acted as if she were an unnecessary burden, but at night she was still 'Mommy'.

She fed the fish, tapping a fingernail on the side of the aquarium to call them to their unexpected midnight snack, and thought about how empty her life would be if it were not filled with Jeremy. She shuddered as she thought about the long discussions she had had with her doctor about abortion. She had considered it seriously; it would have been by far the easiest way. If a girl was unlucky enough to find herself pregnant and alone, she had few options; if she had an abortion, that part of her life could be put behind her forever.

It had been a night much like this one when her decision had been made, she thought as she left Jeremy's room and went out on to the terrace. She'd paced the flagstones for hours in the late summer heat, thinking about herself and her baby.

The next morning she had told Rick she was going to keep the baby. 'You're nuts, Bet,' he had announced. 'You're the craziest girl I've ever known. But if keeping the kid is so important to you, at least get yourself a good lawyer so nobody can take him—her—away from you.'

The memory brought a smile. It had been the best advice Rick had ever given her. And the decision had been the right one. If to have Jeremy she had to have been almost unbearably hurt, then she would rather have the hurt and Jeremy than to have remained untouched.

She sat down in a white wicker chair and put her head back against the soft yellow cushion, thinking about how tiny and sweet Jeremy had been when she'd brought him home.

'Thinking pleasant thoughts, Betsy?' Grady came across the terrace. In his dark pullover and slacks, he'd almost merged into the shadows. 'I suspected you might be out here.'

'What are you doing here?'

He considered that. 'Trespassing,' he decided.

'Well, get out. How did you get here, anyway?'

'Jeremy showed me the way down from my terrace. There's a sort of accidental ladder. You come halfway down the fire escape and sort of slither over the banister, and here you are—right behind that potted palm. You do realise that child of yours is the next thing to a monkey? It took me a while to work up my nerve to try it. I'm no cat burglar.'

'I'll have his head! That's dangerous.'

'I don't think he'll do it again.'

'Why wouldn't he?'

'Because I told him not to.' He pulled up a chair.

'You're a dreamer. You don't think that will stop him, do you?'

'I think so. I also told him that he was welcome anytime to use the regular route, but if he takes the shortcut again there will be no more of my housekeeper's home-made doughnuts, sugar cookies, or . . . what else was it he was eating? I can't remember.'

'He ate all of that?'

Grady nodded. 'It was only ten o'clock this morning, or I'm sure he could have put in a better showing.' He put his hands behind his head and propped his feet on the small table in front of Elizabeth's chair. 'Don't blame him; my mother was encouraging him. She seemed to enjoy watching him eat me out of house and home.'

'Your parents were still here?' Elizabeth was upset. 'I assure you, he doesn't generally run wild in the tenants' apartments.'

Grady shrugged. 'Don't get upset; the housekeeper has been delighted to have him. She misses the old days when Jared and I used to consume everything that was in sight, I guess. I'd suggest, by the way, that if you decide to carry out your threat and tell my family that Jeremy is mine, you'd be wise to skip Whit altogether and just go directly to Mother. She'd be so delighted she wouldn't even ask to see his birth certificate. Which I imagine would save you some embarrassment.'

'Thanks for the advice. I'll consider it if I ever decide to make a try at establishing Jeremy in the bosom of your family.' Elizabeth's tone was dry. 'Now if you've said everything you came down for, why don't you go? I'll be happy to let you out the conventional way.'

'Oh, but I haven't said everything. I came down to see if I was to offer congratulations.'

'For what?'

'Did you accept Tom Bradford's proposal?'

'Why do you think he proposed?' she countered. She walked over to the railing.

'Oh, he just had that desperate look a man wears when he's about to jump off the high dive blindfolded and doesn't know if there is water in the pool. He also looked a little downcast when you left, but I don't know if that was because he was sorry he'd been rejected—or regretting that he'd been accepted.'

Elizabeth turned around and uttered a furious little shriek. 'You have a lot of nerve!'

'Yes, I do, don't I? It comes in handy when I want to know something. Is it to be congratulations?'

'You don't congratulate a bride-to-be, anyway, Grady. You give the bride your best wishes, and you congratulate the groom.'

'Not in this case,' he said callously. 'Did you get your man?'

'No. And not because I couldn't have had him, either.'

'I know. But just think of how miserable you'd be, married to your own employee. To say nothing about how miserable the poor slob would be married to you. Refusing him is the best sense you've shown in years, Betsy. He'll thank you before the month is out.' He smiled lazily up at her. 'Don't bother to tell me what a rat I am. You couldn't possibly be original about it.'

Elizabeth turned her back.

'Very small fish, anyway—Tom. I can't imagine you marrying a mere assistant manager in your own hotel.'

'Maybe he's my one true love.'

Grady laughed. 'Betsy, darling, your one true love is anybody who happens along who has both cash and a willingness to believe in miracles—namely that a creature as beautiful as you could have a heart. I can't figure you out. You haven't seen Jared in a couple of days. . .'

'You scared me off. Why waste my time?'

'And Corbin's gone back out of town. . .'

'Oh, I'm sure he'll call as soon as he hears about that cute little gossip column item.'

'Do you suppose that will make him propose?' Grady's voice held nothing more than polite interest.

'You'll be the first to know.'

'Of course I will. Jeremy will keep me posted. He hates him, you know.'

'Is that where you're getting all of your information? Pumping it out of my son?'

Grady raised an eyebrow. 'No pumping necessary, Betsy. He just flows like a little river. All I do is listen.' He stood up. 'I'm sorry I can't accept your invitation to stay longer, but I am going out of town in the morning, so I'd better catch some sleep. Maybe next time.'

'I'll be delighted to see you out.' She led the way through the apartment, her back absolutely straight. She flung the front door open. 'Goodbye!'

But he didn't move. 'Oh, no. Not till I get my goodnight kiss.'

'That'll be never.'

'Then I'm not leaving. Come on, Betsy—one little kiss. It's a small price to pay for getting rid of me for two days. I'm sure there are things you've paid a higher price for.'

'You're disgusting.'

'I mean it.' He reached out to toy with the single

diamond suspended on a gold chain around her neck. 'Like this, perhaps. A little token of love from one of your men?'

Something impelled her to tell the truth. 'It was a Christmas gift from Myles.'

'I'm glad, Betsy.' Something in her face must have softened, for he took it as consent. He pulled her tight against him, his chest hard against her breasts. 'You were always very kissable,' he murmured, and took his time about proving it. His hands wandered over her body, then one came to cup her breast. The warmth of his hand burned through the thin fabric, bringing a tingle to sensitive nerve endings Elizabeth had sworn were dead. She trembled in his arms, and he smiled and kissed her again, the tip of his tongue gently parting her lips to tease against her teeth. She shivered, and all the resistance melted from her body. Grady groaned, and pulled her even closer, and then there was no more playfulness, just a bone-deep hunger that consumed them both. 'God, you're beautiful, Betsy,' he murmured.

She buried her face in his shoulder. I can still make him want me, she was thinking, a bit vaguely. Then, abruptly, he set her aside. She leaned weakly against the doorframe.

'You know, maybe that gossip columnist had a good idea after all,' he said.

'Oh?' Elizabeth asked faintly. 'The wedding bells or the less formal arrangement?'

There was a wicked glint in his eyes. 'The less formal arrangement, of course,' he said. 'Remember Anne? I'll see you in a couple of days, darling.'

Then he was gone. Elizabeth uttered a muffled oath and picked up a ceramic ashtray from the coffee table. When she threw it, it made a most satisfying crash against the stone of the fireplace.

CHAPTER NINE

JEREMY slid out of the cab, doing his manful best to keep the shopping bag held high enough to clear the street. 'Can we have lunch at the Captain's Table?' he asked Elizabeth. 'You said if I was good and tried on all of the clothes. . .'

'Would you, just once in your life, forget something I promise, instead of forgetting what I tell you to do?' Elizabeth countered. 'And I said we'd do something special. I didn't promise lunch.' She paid the cabdriver and added a generous tip.

'But that's the something special I'd like. Besides, Florence said we were having tuna today.' The disgust in his voice was worthy of the stage.

Elizabeth laughed. 'Very well, Jeremy. But I'll have to call my office and let my secretary know I'll be late.'

'And then they'll call you at least twice during lunch.'

'I am the general manager, dear, and this is my weekend on duty. And there are two conventions coming in this afternoon.'

'You're always on duty.'

'Don't pout or you'll go have tuna. On second thoughts you weren't being very good this morning when I had to come up to the Maxwell and drag you out of the kitchen.'

'Grady's housekeeper makes awful good chocolate-chip cookies,' Jeremy grinned.

'I know. I tasted them. But I wish you'd stop acting as if you belonged up there. What do you talk about, anyway?' It bothered her, what Grady had said last night about Jeremy being a fountain of information. She didn't quite know how to stop that flow—but she was determined not to let it go on.

'We talk about my friends, and baseball, and going to school. Sometimes he tells me about the bank. And Jared teaches me all about computers.'

'Does Grady ask you about me?'

Jeremy wrinkled his nose. 'Why would he want to do that?' he asked. What a waste of time, his tone implied.

'You do my ego wonders, dear,' Elizabeth said. She felt a little better. 'I still don't want you to be up there every day.'

'Grady said I could. He said as long as I come up the regular way. . .' He bit his tongue.

Elizabeth gave him a frosty glare. 'You don't need to act innocent. I already know about your shortcut, and it is being dismantled as soon as the maintenance department can figure out a way to get rid of it.'

'I won't climb it again. Grady told me if I did he'd spank me. And make me stop coming. Would you let him spank me?'

'I certainly would. You're risking your life with that little trick.'

'It's not as dangerous as sitting on the terrace railing. That's twenty-three floors up, and you do it all the time. All I did was climb up to the Maxwell.'

'I know, you were never technically over the street. I don't care, Jeremy. Even one storey is too much. You can stop acting like a monkey and take the elevator—if you must go, which I don't think you need to do. I realise the chocolate-chip-cookie habit is a hard one to break, but you still don't need to be up there every day. Once a week will be plenty.' And no need to have breakfast with Grady every morning, either, though to tell Jeremy that would almost certainly cause a revolt. She tried to tell herself that the housekeeper's cookies—which were certainly good— were the attraction. After all, Grady wasn't even in the city, and Jeremy was still haunting the Maxwell.

'Henry,' she asked the doorman, resplendent in his

maroon livery. 'Would you keep an eye on the trouble-maker here while I make a phone call?'

'I don't need a babysitter,' Jeremy argued.

'In that case, you can be my assistant,' Henry offered.

'Thank you, Henry. Oh, and would you get one of the boys to take these things upstairs?' She indicated Jeremy's shopping bag and her own stack of boxes. 'I can't believe how much stuff a kindergartener needs to start school.'

As she dialled her office, she kept an eye on Jeremy, waiting importantly beside the big doorman. It was surprising how much he already understood of the Englin's operation. She wondered if he would want to run it or if he would choose another career. Rick hadn't liked running the hotel; his tastes had run to much larger operations.

Her secretary answered the phone, and Elizabeth told her, 'I'm going to have lunch at the Captain's Table and then I'll be back in the office. What do I have scheduled for this afternoon?' As the girl reeled off her list of appointments, Elizabeth's eyes roamed the lobby area. Behind the reservation desk, the clerk and the new assistant manager, Jill, were talking to a large man who was getting louder by the minute. No, Elizabeth corrected herself, they were arguing with him. She cut her secretary off in midsentence. 'Unless there's something very important in the messages, I'll take care of them when I get up there.' She cradled the phone and walked across the lobby to the reservation desk.

Jill saw her coming, and Elizabeth read the relief in her eyes. It was her first week on floor duty after completing her training, and Elizabeth felt nothing but sympathy for her. No matter how much experience the girl had, or how good a job Tom had done in training her, the first weeks would be rough. 'Is there something I can help with?' Elizabeth asked.

The man turned to her. 'Do I have to go through it all again?' he said loudly. 'Who in the hell are you?'

'I'm Mrs Englin, the general manager. If you'd like to tell me what's wrong. . .'

'Well, at last! I keep telling these two idiot females they've made a mistake, and they won't listen. I called and made a reservation, and now when I come in to register, they can't find it. I want a room, and I want it now!'

'What is your name, sir?'

'Lawson. Howard Lawson. And I want. . .'

'Of course, sir. Were you with a convention group?'

'No, just a weekend in the city. And it's all starting off wrong, that's for sure. Just you see if I ever come to this hotel again!'

But Elizabeth wasn't listening. Her fingers were flying over the computer keyboard, checking all the possible listings. She even checked to see if the reservation had been made for Lawson Howard. But nothing was listed. Well, whoever had made the mistake, it hadn't been Jill or the reservation clerk. Then something about the man began to seem familiar. The bluster was too blustery.

The reservations clerk leaned over Elizabeth's shoulder. 'Shall I book him in?' she asked quietly. 'There's that block of rooms you saved for the conventions, and no reservations for them.'

'Not just yet,' Elizabeth murmured. 'I think we may still need those rooms.' She called up another computer file.

The clerk saw it appear on the screen, and gasped. 'Of all the nerve,' she said.

Elizabeth took her time and read the entire screen. Then she returned to the man at the desk. 'I'm really sorry, Mr Lawson,' she said pleasantly. 'But next time you want to stay at the Englin, you really should write us a letter reserving a room.'

'Are you implying I'm a liar, ma'am?' His voice rose.

She lifted an elegant eyebrow. 'Of course not, Mr Lawson,' she said gently. 'It's just that this is three times this year you've come in, saying you have a reservation, and we haven't been able to find any record of your phone call. It almost makes me wonder if Ma Bell has put a hex on you.'

'But. . .' He started to sputter.

'I'm sorry that we don't have a room available for you. I'm sure our clerk would be delighted to call another hotel and arrange something.' She gave him a dismissing smile and walked away.

She had gone only a few steps when Jill caught up with her. 'How did you know that?' she asked. 'That he was faking about having a reservation.'

'He was too angry. After a while, you'll begin to see a pattern. It happens frequently. And don't feel bad, Jill— the last two times he got a room. At a discount, of course, to show how much we regretted the inconvenience.'

Jill smiled back. 'Thanks. I feel better now. There's one other thing, if I could bother you. Mr Bradford's gone for the day.'

'That's what I'm here for, Jill.'

'There's a credit transaction I wasn't sure of. Would you look at it, please?'

'Of course.' Elizabeth sat down at the assistant manager's desk.

'Here it is. Mrs Englin?' Jill added tentatively.

'Yes?'

'Maybe I shouldn't say anything, but Mr Bradford asked me to go to a concert with him this weekend. I haven't given him an answer—is there any problem with that?' Her voice was hesitant.

Elizabeth's pen paused over the slip of paper. She could almost hear the words Jill hadn't spoken—if you want him, Mrs Englin, I'll keep my hands off.

'Jill, there's never been any formal policy about employees socialising outside working hours. Just don't let it affect your job.'

There was an instant of silence. 'Of course not.'

And that answer leaves her squarely in the same situation, Elizabeth scolded herself. She'd like to date him, but she thinks she might be risking her job if she does. Might even have risked it by bringing the subject up. If you don't want him, Elizabeth, she told herself firmly, at least make it plain that he is free. She signed her initials firmly at the bottom of the credit slip, looked up, and smiled. 'That's the official statement, Jill. Personally, I'm delighted. I think you might be just what Tom needs right now.' She stood up. 'If you need anything else, I'll be in the Captain's Table.'

She looked around and panicked for an instant when she saw no small shadow beside Henry at the door. Then she spotted Jeremy halfway across the lobby and her heart-beat slowed. It was one of her greatest fears that one day she would turn to look for him and he would not be there. A fear compounded, she supposed, by Rick's sudden death. But Jeremy wasn't alone, and her step faltered for an instant until she identified the broad-shouldered man talking to the small boy. Then she took a deep breath and walked straight to him, noting the appreciative glint in his eyes.

'Hello, Jared,' she said calmly.

'Hi, Mom,' Jeremy chimed in. 'Jared's going to the Captain's Table too, and I asked him to sit with us. He can, can't he, Mom? Please?'

'Of course—if you'd like, Jared. And if you're willing to take your chances with Grady in case he finds out.'

Jared smiled. 'How did you know he'd warned me off?'

'It seemed like the sort of thing he'd do. He's been challenging every man I've spoken to in the last ten days.'

'I don't want to interrupt a family discussion.'

'You won't. And the Captain's Table is usually crowded; they hate to have half-empty tables.'

'In that case, I'd like to join you. It's pleasant to have some friendly faces after a couple of days of meals with clients or alone. The kid here has saved my sanity at breakfast the last couple of mornings.'

'I should think it would be pleasant to be alone. I've certainly been enjoying Grady's absence.' Elizabeth's voice was a little sharper than she had intended.

Jared shot a look at her as he held her chair. 'He has been a little touchy. But don't enjoy it too much; he'll be back this evening.'

'What a pity. It's been so peaceful the last two days. No one throwing insults at me, or assaulting me in my own living room.' Elizabeth opened the menu and missed the expression on Jared's face. 'I should have expected that he'd be gone right now. Everybody in Chicago wants to know why that gossip columnist picked on us for that juicy titbit, and Grady is off God knows where.'

'Milwaukee.'

'Thanks. I didn't want to know. So I'm getting the flak, and he still thinks it was a joke.'

'Maybe you should take it that way, too, Elizabeth.'

'No, thanks, I never did appreciate being the target of gossip.'

Jared glanced over his menu and closed it. 'You should have played golf with us Sunday. It was an interesting round.'

'I wish I had. At least I'd have had a couple of chaperons. Jared, what can I do to get him to leave me alone?'

'I don't know. Ignore him, I suppose.'

'Do you know how hard he is to ignore?'

'Maybe that was a stupid suggestion; I remember trying to ignore him the year he was ten and I was twelve.'

'I can't wait for his lease to be up; I have to get him out of here before that, or I'll be insane.'

'Are you really sure you want him to go away, Elizabeth? I think you're giving him conflicting signals.'

'If I never see your brother again, it will be just dandy with me. No—there's one occasion I won't miss. I shall dance at his wedding with great exhilaration.' She gave her order to the waitress, waited until Jeremy and Jared had done the same, and said, 'When's the happy date, anyway? Grady won't tell me.'

'I imagine he'll have to consult the bride about that,' Jared said, lazily stirring his coffee.

Elizabeth added sugar to her own. 'I hope she doesn't wait too long. Though half the fun of the coup will be in watching all of the society figures anticipate the big event. I imagine Anne will wring every drop of excitement out of it.' She sipped her coffee. 'It'll be the wedding of the century.'

'Elizabeth, you're overdoing it.'

'That's right—put the blame for it on me. It's all my fault that he walks over me. Believe me, Jared, the only interest I take in Grady's romance is this: once he's married, he'll darn well have to leave me alone.'

'Knowing my brother as I do, I would not bet on it.' The waitress returned with Jeremy's milk, and Jared asked her to refill his coffee cup. His smile had a predictable effect on the girl. After the cup was filled and the waitress had gone off starry-eyed, Elizabeth accused, 'You've ruined that girl for the rest of the day. You're the only one who'll get service in her area from now on.'

Jared shrugged. 'Don't blame me.'

'I know, it runs in the family.' She set her cup down and leaned imploringly across the table. 'Jared, isn't there something you can do? At least tell your parents that it just isn't going to work to push us together. Grady has his Anne, and I have. . .'

'What do you have? It would take a lot to convince them that you prefer being single to marrying Grady. I know he's a pain in the neck sometimes, but he does look a lot like the answer to a maiden's prayer.' He folded his arms on the edge of the table. 'It would also be difficult to make Whit and Mother understand why they should prefer Anne to you as a daughter-in-law.'

'Jared, you don't know how funny that is. At any rate, you don't need to tell them Anne would make a better member of the family, though no doubt she would, once she grows up. Just tell them that it is impossible that Grady and I will ever be anything but adversaries. And if you could drop a hint to Myles, that would help too. I'm just too old to have a couple of matchmaking families after me.'

Jared's expression became alarmed. 'Don't tell Grady you think they're matchmaking, for Pete's sake!'

'He told me. He thinks it's funny. And why shouldn't I tell him what I think, anyway?'

'Because we don't need another family rift. The last one took five years to patch up.'

The waitress set Elizabeth's shrimp salad in front of her. 'Ugh, rubber band salad,' Jeremy remarked before digging into his own lasagne.

Elizabeth picked up her fork. 'The Captain's Table has the best shrimp salad in the Loop,' she told Jeremy. He merely wrinkled his nose disapprovingly and stretched out a strand of cheese with his fork.

Jared laughed. 'That sounds like a longstanding argument.'

'It is,' Elizabeth assured him. 'Children don't start to develop good taste in food until they become teenagers.' Her mind was still on Jared's comment. She'd known there was some sort of mystery about Grady and his father. A family rift? Because Whit was matchmaking? It didn't sound like the whole story. There certainly had appeared to be no strain the evening that Whit and Helene had been there. The Logans had laughed and joked, and there hadn't seemed to be any subjects that were taboo, as if to get too close to them would be to court another outbreak· of hostilities. She would have said they were about as close as parents and a grown son could be.

Her eyes rested pensively on her son. 'Jeremy, you have a milk moustache. Use your napkin, dear.' She looked at her shrimp salad without interest. 'And stop playing with the cheese on that lasagne or it's the last time you'll have lunch down here. Jared, you and Grady are the only two children, aren't you?'

'Yes. And what about you?'

'What do you mean?'

'Was Rick your brother or your cousin?'

'I wondered how long it would take you to put two and two together,' Elizabeth murmured. 'Somehow I expected you'd know it right away. He was my brother.'

'Younger sisters were not a large part of our conversations at the frat house,' Jared said dryly. 'Especially if they were young enough to be out of the running as dates. Or perhaps it was just that Rick didn't trust any of us.' He took a thoughtful bite of his quiche. 'Maybe I should tell Grady that.'

'I wish you wouldn't.'

'Does he still think you were married to Rick?'

'Unless someone has told him differently.'

'Don't look at me. But it might improve his temper if I told him. Why have you let him go on thinking that?'

Elizabeth pushed her plate away and waited while the waitress refilled her cup. 'It was easier than telling him the truth.'

'Which is?'

She looked at him impassively.

Finally he said, 'I'm not going to go running to him with

the whole story, Elizabeth. I didn't tell him that you weren't married to Rick, did I? Trust me.'

'Why should I? He's your brother.'

'For some insane reason—I suppose because of the way I felt about Rick—I keep thinking you're my sister. And because I'm having too much fun watching Grady make a damn fool of himself to want to interfere.'

'That's gratifying.' She sipped her coffee. 'I didn't think it was any of Grady's business. Jeremy, if you've finished playing with that lasagne, go back up to the apartment, please. And have Florence call my office when you get there.'

'I always get sent away when you start talking about something interesting,' Jeremy complained, but he got down from his chair.

'I'll see you tomorrow, Jared.'

'Wouldn't miss it for the world, pal.' He watched the child leave the restaurant. 'Well, Elizabeth?'

Obviously he would not accept evasion. She sighed, and said, 'I married very young and very foolishly. My husband was not the sort of person I thought he was; he enjoyed inflicting pain. The marriage lasted less than a month. I came back home, Rick got me an annulment, and I resumed my maiden name. In the middle of all that I realised I was pregnant. I became Mrs Englin for convenience.' She shrugged. 'That's Elizabeth Englin in a nutshell. I don't like to talk about Jeremy's father to him; he isn't old enough to understand. And since all of Chicago has grown to accept me for what I am, and all of the old scandal has died down, I didn't want to drag it all out of the closet for Grady's enjoyment. It was easier to let him think I'd married Rick for his money.'

Jared shook his head. 'It looks to me as if you've just bought yourself some extra trouble with that story. After all, it isn't as bad as it would have been if you weren't married at all.'

'No, it isn't.'

'When he finds out, he'll be really angry.'

'Why should he be angry? It's none of his business. And how will he find out, if you don't tell him?'

'Too many people know. Don't worry, I will keep your deep, dark secret. But don't underestimate Grady. He's no dunce, you know. Under that stubborn surface is a very keen mind, if he ever chooses to put it to work on you.'

Elizabeth pushed a bit of salad around on her plate with a fork. 'You mentioned a family rift,' she said finally, curiosity overwhelming her. 'What happened? Grady told me he's been in Denver for several years.'

'Whit made the supreme mistake—he tried to tell that hard-headed Dutchman what to do. Grady got himself mixed up with a very unsuitable woman, and Whit told him to cut himself loose. That's why I don't want it to even cross Grady's mind that Whit would like to push him into marriage. Which Whit would, of course.'

'What did Grady do?'

'He told Whit to go to hell, resigned from the banks, came out to Denver, and used my company to get a foothold in the banking business out there. Five years later he was a tycoon in his own right—as I warned you, he does have a brilliant mind—and when he rejoined the family banks, he did it as a full partner.'

Elizabeth crumbled a cracker. 'What about the woman?'

Jared groaned. 'Thus speaks the female mind. You women always want to find out how the fair sex turned out. It hardens my resolve to never get married. As far as I know, he never saw her again. Which is where the hard-headedness comes in, you see, because he didn't speak to Whit for five years.'

'I see. She must have been something special to cause a rift like that.'

Jared shook his head. 'No, I think Grady was looking

for an excuse. He wanted to prove to himself that he could make it without Whit's backing. He'd have picked a fight over something else if Whit hadn't been short-sighted enough to make an issue out of her.'

'You're no doubt right. You do know him well, don't you?'

'You can get to know a lot about a person in thirty years. Does Jeremy's father ever see him?'

'I never caught up with the man long enough to tell him he had a son. To be perfectly honest, I didn't try very hard.'

'Perhaps I'm out of line to say anything at all—but do you think that's fair to Jeremy? He wants his father, Elizabeth. He talks about him a lot, you know.'

'Children want a lot of things, but they don't always get them.' Her voice was cold. It was an argument she had had with herself many times. Perhaps she should let Jeremy know his father, but if he was rejected, she didn't know if he could accept that. He was very young yet to understand how the human mind could work sometimes.

'This is hardly the same thing as wanting every game that's advertised on TV, Elizabeth,' Jared pointed out. When she didn't answer, he sighed. 'I suppose you know best. I'd better go—I have a lot of loose ends to tie up this afternoon.'

'Are you going home soon?'

'Yes, I'm just wrapping everything up, so I can go back to Denver tomorrow. Do you have the weekend off?'

'No, I've had the last two, so I'm on call this weekend. And we have two conventions coming in this afternoon, so it will no doubt be a busy couple of days.'

'That's the worst of being the boss, isn't it?' He picked up the bill. 'Thanks for having lunch with me.'

'On—let me get that,' Elizabeth protested. 'Jeremy didn't invite you to lunch so we could make you pay the bill.'

Jared laughed. 'Sorry, but my father taught me never to let a lady pay for anything. Perhaps I'll be liberated someday—about the same time I meet that one woman whom you so fondly believe will change my mind about marriage. You really are a romantic at heart, aren't you, Elizabeth?'

'She'll be a brunette,' Elizabeth predicted.

'Oh, no. The only weak spot I have is for redheads.' He leered, à la Groucho Marx, and stroked his moustache. 'Sorry to disappoint you, dear, but she will never be a brunette.'

Elizabeth shook her head. 'I just hope I'm there to jeer when you walk up the aisle.'

'Stick with Grady and you will be,' Jared advised. 'He'll have to be my best man. Maybe you can be a bridesmaid. But don't hold your breath about when it will happen.'

Elizabeth stirred her coffee absently as she watched him leave the restaurant. She should go back to her office, she knew, but she continued to sit, her chin propped on one hand, the other idly stirring the coffee. And when she lifted the cup and drank, she didn't notice that the liquid was cold, because she wasn't really there. She was back in a little inn in a tiny town in Wisconsin, on a July evening more than five years before.

It had been her evening to work the reception desk. That was one of the reasons she liked her job, because she got to do everything. It was the best way to learn the hotel business; Myles had told her that. He'd started out as a bellboy at the Englin when he was in his teens; his father had insisted that a person who hadn't worked all of the jobs on his way up could never be a good manager.

Rick had done the same, working in most of the hotel's departments before he was out of his teens. But Myles hadn't wanted Elizabeth to learn the business. No matter how she had begged to join the housekeeping department for her first job, he had refused.

Elizabeth had given up the idea that she would ever persuade him that a woman could run the Englin—or the Englin chain, if she chose. Showing Myles would be the only way the stubborn old man would be convinced. And that was why, that summer when she was halfway through college, she had told him she was spending the summer with the family of a friend, and had gone to work in Bridgedale.

She had used her mother's name and had avoided personal conversations with the other employees, in an effort to keep secret the fact that she was a member of the Englin family. Being an impostor, she'd learned, was no fun. The other girls thought she was stuck-up, and soon left her alone. Some thought she was a crawler because she was always volunteering for extra work. Like the reception desk—which wasn't part of her job. But Elizabeth wanted to see how everything operated, so when the chance came she grabbed at it.

That was how it had happened that Betsy Ames was at the reception desk the evening Grady Logan had checked in.

It was almost sunset, and the stained glass fanlight over the big front door cast jewelled puddles of brilliant light over the floor, the desk, and Elizabeth. The light streaming over her always annoyed her, and she was standing with a hand raised to protect her eyes. When Grady came in, he stopped for a second to stare at her, and Elizabeth's breath caught.

It wasn't that he was exceptionally handsome, because he wasn't. There was an aura about him, though, an air of power and energy that was stronger than any she had ever sensed before.

She fumbled with the registration card and felt like a teenager on a first date. And she was disappointed when he simply filled the card out and handed it back.

She glanced at the card. 'I hope you enjoy your stay with us, Mr Logan,' she said.

'I'm certain I will, Miss. . .' He read her name tag. 'Miss Betsy Ames. How sweet.' He took his room key from her and swung it playfully. 'I'll be out by the pool later, when you're looking for me.'

'Looking for you?' Elizabeth sputtered. 'What makes you think I'll come looking for you?'

'You will,' he promised softly, and left the lobby.

And, of course, she did. She tried not to let herself believe it; she told herself that she only wanted a swim and that it was unfair not to be able to have it just because some conceited guest thought he was irresistible. But whatever the reason, she was beside the pool, stretched out on a towel pretending to be asleep, when he pulled himself out of the water.

'Hi,' he said.

She ignored him. She was lying on her back, her head turned away from him.

'I thought you'd be here. It took you a while to make up your mind, though,' he said.

'There was nothing to make up my mind about. I just decided to have a swim.'

There was an instant of silence. Then, suddenly, he picked her up. Elizabeth found herself cradled in his arms, unable to escape. She thrashed about, but he held her easily.

'Put me down!' she demanded.

'I'm sorry, I don't hear very well. Did you come out here to find me?'

'No. I told you—I decided to take a swim.'

'Okay,' he said obligingly and took two steps towards the pool.

By the time Elizabeth realised what he was going to do, she was airborne. She had only a moment to grab a breath before she hit the water with a gigantic splash. She surfaced, sputtering, to find him treading water beside her.

'Why did you come out here?' he demanded.

'To find you,' she said meekly.

'That's what I thought.' He struck out for the side of the pool.

When Elizabeth climbed out, he tossed her towel at her. 'Let's find someplace a little more private,' he ordered. 'I wouldn't want to get you in trouble with your boss.'

'How thoughtful,' she mocked.

He stopped rubbing his hair dry and glanced curiously at her. 'You sound as if you need another dunking,' he said. 'And you might as well know right now that I intend to make love to you. Not tonight, perhaps—but I will.'

Elizabeth laughed at him. 'You don't know anything about me. And I don't know anything about you.'

'What do you want to know?' He took her arm, still rubbing his hair with the towel. It stood up in wet, brown peaks. 'I don't need to know anything more about you. You're a woman who needs the firm hand of a man to keep you under control. Where shall we go?'

'Thanks, but I think I'm going back to my room.'

'I play fair, Betsy. I don't take advantage of anybody. I told you straight out what I want to do—how much fairer can I be? Or are you just chicken?'

So she went. And the next day, which happened to be her day off, she spent with him. He made love to her that night as he had promised he would, gently and slowly, taking her to heights she had never dreamed existed.

They had two weeks, days in which Elizabeth did her work absently while Grady negotiated banking policies for his father, evenings when they played, nights of love that left them exhausted but never satiated.

On the fourteenth day, Elizabeth finished her work and started back to her room to shower and dress so that she would be ready when Grady came. The girl at the reception desk stopped her as she passed through the lobby.

'Your boy-friend called,' she said. 'I offered to come and find you, but he said he didn't have time. So he just left a message.'

Elizabeth put a hand to her throat. 'What is it?'

The girl studied a slip of paper, drawing out the agony. 'He had to go back to New York.'

'Is that all?'

'He said he'd call. But if it was me—I wouldn't count on it.'

'He'll call,' Elizabeth had said, but it was more a prayer than a conviction. He'd told her that he played fair, and he did. At no time had he promised her anything more than a good time.

Of course, he didn't call. Three weeks later Rick called her to tell her Myles had had a heart attack. She went home in a daze, as she had lived that last three weeks, still not believing that she had invested so much of herself in a man who had cared so little.

Ironically, of course, Myles' illness had left him unable to manage the hotel, and Elizabeth stepped in. By the time he was out of the hospital, she was entrenched as the general manager. He'd never even asked her why she thought she could do it.

Elizabeth took another sip of her coffee and grimaced. She pushed the cup aside and left the Captain's Table, and as she walked through the big lobby she reminded herself that no matter what, the Englin would always be there. People could not be relied on, but the Englin would never fail her.

CHAPTER TEN

ELIZABETH peeked in the door of the Grand Ballroom. So far, everything there was peaceful. The speaker at the rostrum thundered as he made the keynote speech for the convention. The applause must have pleased him, for he stood with his head bowed humbly for a few seconds before continuing.

Under cover of the noise, Elizabeth stepped back out into the hall. With that group happily settled at last, her day's work was done. She glanced at the gold clock on the mezzanine and sighed. Almost eleven. It had been a very long afternoon. She'd been right, at lunch, when she had told Jared it would be a busy weekend.

She strolled down the grand staircase and started towards the Library Lounge. She didn't want to bother Myles with the details of the day, but if she didn't unwind before going up to the apartment, she was certain to. What a way for a weekend to start! she told herself. One convention, by itself, was all right. But when there were two, and neither understood why it couldn't have the entire hotel at its disposal, it was bound to be an unpleasant weekend for everybody.

The reception desk was quiet. At one point this afternoon it had been twenty-people deep. One of the conventions, it seemed, had told its members that reservations weren't needed. Only Elizabeth's instinctive action in holding back that block of rooms had saved her neck, and even so she had had to shuttle part of them up the street to a sister hotel. Some of the conventioneers hadn't been happy. In the middle of the mess, the president of the organisation had threatened to move the entire convention to a suburb. Elizabeth had been within an inch of begging him to do that.

She let the dim coolness of the Library Lounge settle around her. A fire flickered behind glass doors in the huge fireplace, and in front of it sat Tonya and Alan McConnell. Tonya saw her and waved.

'Hi, stranger. Come on over,' she invited, and indicated a chair. 'You look as if you could use a drink.'

'I could, at that. Am I intruding on a party?'

'Heavens, no. I'm just hoping somebody really important will come in and recognise you so they'll think I'm a big shot sitting here with the general manager,' Tonya teased.

'If anyone comes in that door looking even vaguely as if he wants to talk to me, I will crawl under the table. A Manhattan, please,' she told the waitress. The girl nodded.

'It's busy enough tonight, isn't it?' Alan asked. 'We were lucky to get a reservation for dinner.'

'We have two conventions,' Elizabeth nodded. 'Each of which seems to think it has exclusive rights. And one of them is the Midwest cigarette distributors group and the other one is the Anti-Lung Cancer League. They haven't been willing to co-operate.'

'Drink up,' Alan advised as the waitress returned.

The girl set three drinks down and, holding a fourth, looked questioningly at Alan. 'The other gentleman. . .' she began.

'He went to make a phone call. Just put it down.' The waitress nodded and did so.

'You do have a party,' Elizabeth apologised. 'I'm sorry.'

'Oh, it's nothing formal. We just ran into him when we came in after dinner.' Tonya sipped her wine. 'Here he comes now.'

Elizabeth didn't turn to look at the entrance directly

behind her chair. She didn't have to. The hair prickling on the back of her neck told her who was coming across the room. Well, Jared had told her Grady would be back tonight. What black magic was it that made him turn up wherever she went?

Grady pulled out the fourth chair and sat down. 'The scenery has changed since I left,' he remarked, running an appraising eye over Elizabeth. 'You really shouldn't wear black, Betsy. It makes you look as if you're in mourning.'

'I suppose that makes you nervous. That's your problem, not mine.'

The sapphire eyes summed her up—the thin jersey of her dress, with its demure long sleeves and unadorned neckline, the fair hair swept up into a classic knot, and the green eyes shadowed now from the long day.

Elizabeth ignored his scrutiny. As she reached for her drink the firelight caught the polished gold of the ring on her left hand, and she could have sworn that Grady not only noticed it but had to force himself not to say whatever it was that hovered on his tongue. She sent a direct, cold look at him and turned to Tonya. 'I think I'll take Jeremy to the Cubs game on Sunday. Would Brian like to go?'

'He'd love it. I'll answer for him.'

'Let's consider it a date, then. Would you like to go shopping one day next week? There's a new little boutique up on Wabash—I looked in the window this morning while I was shopping for school clothes for Jeremy. But he wouldn't have stood still for me trying anything on, so I didn't even go in.'

'Do you have all of Jeremy's things? I'm still trying to get in the mood to buy Brian's.'

'Don't wait too long. It takes forever to find everything. Shall we check out the boutique?'

'Sounds good. My autumn wardrobe needs some help.'

Alan groaned. 'So does my budget.'

Tonya sent him a disgusted-wife look.

Grady sipped his drink. 'Just stick to green, Betsy,' he advised. 'It's by far your best colour.'

The day had been just a little too long for Elizabeth. 'Mr Logan, I will buy what I want to buy, and if I want to show up here in purple velvet with gold metallic polka dots that is absolutely none of your business.' She waved a contemptuous hand. 'And as long as we're talking about black—it makes you look like an undertaker.'

She had to admit that wasn't quite true. Grady in dinner clothes looked nothing like an undertaker. The pent-up energy that seeped from him was hardly the restful quality one would expect from a mortician.

Grady didn't appear to hear the jibe. 'Gold metallic polka dots,' he mused. 'Are you planning to run off and join the circus? Or are you just making a protest statement because you've lost another boy-friend? Bradford just came in with a new girl on his arm.'

'Tom?' Tonya twisted around in her seat. 'Elizabeth, I can't believe it. Who is she?'

Elizabeth waved at Jill. 'My newest assistant manager. And despite Grady's difficulty in believing me, I'm thrilled.'

'Oh, I believe you could have had him if you'd really wanted him. But I can't see you being thrilled that he's consoled himself so quickly.' He raised his glass.

Tonya tapped her ring against the side of her glass. 'That's enough, both of you,' she scolded. 'Now behave yourselves, or I'll send you both to your rooms.'

'That's the best idea I've heard all day,' Elizabeth's voice was enthusiastic. 'Tonya—Alan—I really am tired, and I'm on call all weekend. I'll see you later. What day would you like to go shopping?'

'I'll call you,' Tonya promised. 'But I didn't mean to make you leave. . .'

'Believe me, dear, it wasn't you,' Elizabeth assured her. She ignored Grady completely and left the room.

He caught up with her in the elevator lobby. 'Oh, no,' she protested. 'If I haven't made myself clear enough about wanting to be alone. . .'

'But I don't want to be alone; I want to be with you,' he pointed out, as if that solved anything. 'Betsy, you never cease to amaze me. It is so incredibly easy to get you to do exactly what I want. If I'd been polite and charming to you, we'd have been tied up with social gatherings half the night. So I make a couple of smart remarks, and you promptly get up and leave. And you even gave me the perfect out. All I had to do was look stricken and beg to be excused so that I could apologise to you.'

'Which of course you have no intention of doing.'

'Of course not. I didn't say a thing I didn't mean.'

Elizabeth sighed and leaned wearily against the wall. An elevator across the lobby discharged a carload of conventioneers. She looked at them with well-disguised loathing and said, 'I am not sharing an elevator with you. Why don't you just run along up like a good boy?'

'And I'm not going until you come along. We'll look a bit foolish standing here in evening clothes when the breakfast crowd starts coming down.'

Elizabeth gave in. 'Is there anything you won't do to get your own way?'

'Nothing. I'm glad you're beginning to realise that. It will save me a great deal of trouble when I tell you you're going to marry me.'

Elizabeth wasn't sure if the jolt in the region of her heart was caused by his announcement or the jerk of the elevator as it started up. 'What did you say?' she asked faintly.

'You heard me.'

'You said you were going to marry Anne.'

'You were right; Anne's only a child. And I didn't say I was going to marry her. You asked if I was thinking of getting married, and I said I was. I didn't confide the name of the lady. A gentleman never does.'

'You aren't a gentleman.' Elizabeth sat down on the bench and leaned her head against the brass rail. She must really be tired, she thought, if that felt like a pillow.

'You force me to tell you that you aren't a lady, either. It's the only solution I can come up with, you see. I feel a certain obligation to protect the rest of the male population from your fatal charm, but exactly how to do that is the problem. Then I hit upon marriage. It will keep you busy enough that your time to look around will be limited. Plus, I think it would take a very unusual man to fall into your web, knowing that you have a husband who'll make mincemeat out of anybody who trespasses on his territory.'

'You've flipped.' The elevator whooshed to a halt. 'I'll forget this conversation ever happened.'

'I wouldn't if I were you. Because I always get what I want.' He followed her out of the car and took the key from her suddenly nerveless hand.

'And you want me? Why am I not flattered?'

He opened the door and gave her a blinding smile. 'Darling, what man in his right mind wouldn't want you?'

Elizabeth glanced around the darkened living room, her last hope for rescue fading as she realised Myles was not there. She would have to bluff her own way out of this. 'Now that you've seen me safely home, goodnight,' she said calmly. 'I'll definitely consider your ... suggestion. . .'

'"Proposal" is the accepted term,' he interrupted.

'Suggestion—and I'll let you know tomorrow what my answer is.'

'Your answer. . .' He captured her hand and traced the heart line with the tip of his tongue. 'Your answer will be yes.'

'And how did you come to that conclusion?' Elizabeth

willed her voice to be firm, but it came out in a whisper.

'Because you're a very passionate creature, Betsy, and the only way you're going to be happy is with a man who's stronger than you are—a man who can see through your little games. A man who's strong enough not to fall in love with you—because if he ever does you'll have the upper hand over him, and he'll never again have a moment's peace.' His hands cupped her face and turned it up to his.

'And you think I'll find this strong man irresistible?'

'I think you'll find this irresistible.' Slowly he drew her closer to him.

'Please, Grady, don't. . .'

He ignored her protest and set about kissing her with a slow sensuality that sent flame licking along her veins. She drew a deep, shuddering breath, and Grady smiled in lazy satisfaction and kissed her again.

Time passed—long ecstatic minutes in which Elizabeth forgot his boast that he would never love her, minutes in which the only thing of importance was his embrace. He raised his head a fraction and demanded huskily, 'Give me your answer now, Betsy. Say yes now.'

And she murmured, 'Yes,' and his lips crushed hers again, demanding a response that she was only too glad to give, his hands exploring every curve with the familiar intimacy of a beloved husband.

The little voice tugged at a corner of her mind, but it took a couple of cries before Elizabeth really heard it. Then, suddenly, it was as if somebody had drenched her in cold water, and she heard Jeremy cry, 'Mommy!'

She wrenched herself out of Grady's arms.

'What's the matter?' he asked.

'Jeremy's calling for me. He's probably having a nightmare.' She started down the hall. 'Would you let yourself out?'

But he followed her. 'I'm not leaving until I've got that answer down in writing.'

'I don't plan to be held responsible for something said when I was not in full control,' Elizabeth said tartly.

'Just think how embarrassing it will be if I have to kiss you into submission in front of the whole crowd at our wedding. And don't bother to tell me I couldn't do it,' he added.

But Elizabeth wasn't listening. Just then her whole mind was on Jeremy, who was sitting up in bed, arms outstretched, tears streaming down his face, flushed and burning up with fever.

'Do nightmares generally affect him like this?' Grady asked.

'Of course not.' She put gentle arms around her son. 'Would you bring a cool washcloth from the bathroom? It's next door. And there should be some calamine lotion there, too.'

'Some what?'

'Calamine lotion. To stop the itching.' She stroked Jeremy's hair, and added, 'I hope you've had chicken pox, Grady, because you've now been exposed.'

'You're hoping I haven't, and you know it. But you're out of luck. There isn't anything Jared and I didn't have.'

'Darn.' But Grady was already gone.

The remedies helped for a few minutes, but as Jeremy's temperature went back up, he became increasingly fussy.

'He's exhausted,' Grady said finally. 'If he would just stay still for a few minutes, he'd go to sleep automatically.'

'Do you want to try holding him down?' Elizabeth asked tartly. She was sitting on the edge of Jeremy's bed, rubbing his back, and her spine was beginning to cramp. It was now after midnight.

'Why not?' Grady asked. 'I'll try my hand at anything once. It looks to me as if you're going to have a long night of it. Why don't you go change into something more comfortable while I see what I can do?'

Elizabeth hesitated before accepting the olive branch,

but she knew from experience that she'd be up all night or until Jeremy's fever broke. 'All right,' she said. 'I'll just be a minute.'

Once in her room, she pulled the pins from her hair in relief and let the blonde waves cascade around her shoulders. She sank on to the bench in front of her dressing table and laid her head on her arms, careless of the cosmetics that lay on the glass top. If Grady thought he could do so much, she thought, let him have a fair chance to try. She was so exhausted that she could fall into bed and sleep for a week. If she could only escape from everything that was on her mind right now, she would take Jeremy and go away. But what good would it do to go away when the problems would go with her—or be waiting for her when she returned?

She wearily got to her feet and pulled on an old cotton nightgown and a terry bathrobe. It wasn't a designer-fashioned costume—in fact, it could charitably be called 'serviceable'—but it couldn't get her into trouble, even with Grady, she concluded as she went back down the hall.

Jeremy's room was silent. Unbelieving, she tiptoed in. Grady was sitting in the rocker, a blanket-wrapped Jeremy on his lap. And the child, blessedly, was asleep.

'Did I say something about you having a long night ahead?' Grady asked in an undertone.

'Maybe if you put him down very carefully. . .'

He shook his head. 'I don't want to take the chance. And it really isn't uncomfortable at all. If you would just take off my tie—I do have both hands occupied.'

'Of course.' Elizabeth tugged on the bow tie, laid it aside, and unfastened the top button on his shirt.

'Thanks. That helps a lot.'

Elizabeth sat down on the edge of the bed.

'He's really paranoid about being sick, isn't he?' Grady asked.

Instantly she was defensive. 'You try being sick from the day you're born, and see what happens to you. Anything he gets is always worse than when anybody else has it.'

'Is there something wrong with him?'

'No. He's growing out of it—just a tendency he's had. Did it suddenly occur to you that if you marry me you'll be responsible for Jeremy? Is that the reason for this touching concern?' She paced the room. 'Well, you don't need to worry, because I have no intention of marrying you, ever.'

'Be quiet.'

'I wouldn't marry you if you were the last man on earth!'

'That wasn't what I meant. Just don't wake the kid up. And if I were you, Betsy, I wouldn't say that too loudly. Somebody is apt to throw it up at you on our wedding day.'

'What does it take to convince you that I mean what I said?'

'I happen to think you meant what you said an hour ago when you said yes. And if I didn't have my arms full already I'd prove it to you.'

Elizabeth backed away instinctively.

Grady grinned. 'I see you think I can do it.'

'I'd just like to know what makes you believe I'd be foolish enough to marry you.'

'Because I think you're a little tired of the game. The sport has gone out of it. You're reaching the age when you'd prefer respectability to almost anything else, assuming that it has money to go with it. I have plenty of money, I'm perfectly respectable, and you know darn well we'd have fun.'

He shifted Jeremy slightly and watched Elizabeth. When she didn't answer, he continued, 'Besides, I could blackmail you to death right now. Rumour has it that you weren't married to Rick.'

'Oh? Did Jared tell you that?'

'Does Jared know it?' he countered. 'As a matter of fact, Vicki Andrews told me.'

'And what else did she confide about me?'

'Nothing. Not that she wasn't willing to; I just thought it would be better to let you tell me yourself. Is there anything else I should know?'

'Well, rumour has it right. I wasn't married to Rick.'

'I suspected that. This Mrs Englin business hasn't rung true from the beginning. Was he going to marry you?'

'No.'

'Is Jeremy actually his son?'

'No. Now are you satisfied?'

He shook his head thoughtfully. 'I see only one way out of it, Betsy.'

She looked at him dispassionately. 'What's in it for you? If I'm such a tramp. . .'

He laughed softly. 'Go look in a mirror, Betsy. No, perhaps you'd better wait till morning, when you've had a little sleep. And speaking of sleep. . .' He put his head back on the cushioned rocker and closed his eyes.

'Are you really prepared to spend the night that way?'

He looked up. 'This is hardly an appropriate time to start convincing a frightened child that he isn't going to die of the chicken pox. Go get some sleep. We'll be all right, and frankly, you're in our way here.'

'Give him to me.'

'Elizabeth—' and there was no doubting the order in his voice, 'go hit the sack so you can relieve me at the crack of dawn. Now march!'

The sun was just peeking over the lake when she tiptoed into Jeremy's room again. She didn't know what she expected to find, but it wasn't what she saw. Grady had shed his coat and shoes and was stretched out on Jeremy's bed, one arm casually around the child as if he were a teddy bear. Both of them were sound asleep. Elizabeth put a gentle hand on Jeremy's forehead. It was cool. Smiling, she stooped to drop a kiss on his cheek.

Grady's arm came up around her neck. 'How about one of those for me, too?' he invited.

'I'm all out. It was a small shipment today.'

He laughed. 'I guess I'd rather collect sometime when I don't have a chaperon, anyway.' He extricated his other arm from under Jeremy's head and sat up. 'His fever broke about four, by the way. He's been sound asleep ever since.'

'You should have let me know. There was no need to stay all night.'

'He wouldn't let go of me. He kept saying, "Don't leave me, don't go away." I promised I wouldn't, so I didn't.' There was a question in his eyes. Elizabeth ignored it.

'Hi, Mommy.' Jeremy rubbed his eyes sleepily.

'How are you this morning, Jeremy?'

'Itchy.' It was uncompromising.

'I'll run you a bath and put soda in it to help the itch.'

Grady reached for his shoes. 'I'm going home for breakfast.'

Jeremy's hand shot out and clutched his arm. 'Don't go away,' he said. 'Florence makes breakfast.' His voice was panicky.

Grady ruffled his hair. 'I'm just going upstairs. I'll be back to see how you're doing.'

'When?' It was a sullen question.

'Don't demand, Jeremy. Ask politely, and you'll get an answer.' Grady's voice was firm.

To Elizabeth's utter astonishment, Jeremy said, 'When will you come back to see me?'

'Would later this morning be convenient? We'll let your mother go see how her conventions are doing.'

'Did you have to remind me?' Elizabeth muttered.

'All right.' Jeremy agreed reluctantly. 'If it's a promise.'

Grady held up two fingers. 'Cub Scout's honour.'

'That,' Elizabeth said firmly once they were outside the door, 'was not fair. You're using him.'

Grady, hair ruffled, managed to look like an angel. 'Why not? You were prepared to use him for an excuse for not marrying me. I just spiked your cannon, dear.' He sketched a salute and hurried down the hall, near colliding with Florence as she came out of the dining room.

The housekeeper looked startled, and then puzzled. She looked down the hall and saw Elizabeth leaning against the bathroom door in her robe. A wide smile broke across her face. 'The Lord be praised!' she said.

'Florence!' Elizabeth said between clenched teeth. But the housekeeper merely smiled wider and went back into the kitchen.

Elizabeth shook a fist towards the woman's back and went to run Jeremy's bath and get dressed.

When she was reapplying lotion to soothe his chicken pox, he asked, 'Do I look like my father?'

Elizabeth closed her eyes for a second and counted to ten. If there was one thing she didn't need today, this was it. 'Not today; he didn't have spots.' Maybe if she kept her answers light, he'd give up. 'There you go, all the spots covered.'

Jeremy looked down his body with a sort of pride. 'I bet I've got the biggest case of chicken pox in all Chicago,' he boasted. 'Don't I, Mom?'

'I think you're right up there with the champions, Jeremy. I changed your bed while you were in your bath. How about hopping back in while I go see what's for breakfast?'

'Oh, Mom, it's warm outside. Can I go out on the terrace?'

Elizabeth considered it. 'If you'll stay in a chair and not be running around,' she said finally. 'But you'll have to play quietly.'

'All right.' He pulled on his robe and picked up a plastic bucket of toy soldiers. 'I wonder when Grady will be back.'

Elizabeth settled him in a lounge chair on the terrace. 'I wouldn't hold my breath,' she cautioned.

'But he promised!'

'And I'm sure he means to keep his promise. But something might interfere. It does sometimes, you know.'

He considered that. 'Did my daddy promise he'd come back?'

Elizabeth strangled the urge to scream. 'No, Jeremy, he never promised.'

'He could come back, though. He's not dead.' The child's voice was positive.

'How do you know that?'

'Because I'd know if he was dead. I'd just know.' Jeremy looked at her defiantly, as if challenging her to tell him otherwise.

'Someday you'll understand, Jeremy.' It was the best Elizabeth could do.

When she came into the kitchen, dressed in a halter top, brief shorts, and sandals, Florence looked up with a knowing smile.

'Oh, wipe the leer off your face, Florence,' Elizabeth said crossly. 'And yes, Grady did spend the night here.'

Florence murmured, 'I didn't think he generally put on a dinner jacket at six in the morning. Especially without a tie.'

Elizabeth continued as if she hadn't been interrupted. 'But that doesn't mean he stayed in my room.'

'Maybe if he had you'd be in a better mood. What does his young lordship want for breakfast?'

'Something soft. Eggnog, perhaps.'

Florence started to break eggs. 'He looks as if the termites have been eating on him.'

'What a charming simile. I imagine he feels that way too.'

'Well, cheer up. Chicken pox can't last all that long—even on Jeremy. In a couple of days he'll be getting back to normal.'

'One can always hope. Good morning, Myles.'

'Good morning,' Myles returned cheerfully. 'Is the coffee made, Florence? And what's that you're stirring up?'

'Eggnog. Here's your coffee.'

He tasted it. 'Ah, marvellous this morning. Strong and hot. If you'll fix another cup, Florence, I'll take it out to Grady on the terrace.'

'Is he back already?' It burst out despite Elizabeth's best intentions.

Myles looked surprised. 'Back? What do you mean?'

Florence giggled, then, as Elizabeth shot a look at her, she hastily turned back to the blender, murmuring something about eggnog.

Elizabeth tried to pass it off lightly. 'Jeremy came down with the chicken pox in the middle of the night. Grady ended up holding him most of the night—Jeremy was in no mood to be left alone.'

Myles' eyebrows threatened to disappear over the back of his head, but he said only, 'Chicken pox, hmm? I think perhaps I'll reconsider going on to the terrace. I'll be in my study if anyone needs me.' He stopped at the door and looked back at Elizabeth. 'Chicken pox,' he repeated thoughtfully, and disappeared down the hall.

Elizabeth said a word she generally reserved for moments of high stress.

'Jeremy's toast has popped up,' Florence pointed out. 'What a father-figure for a kid—he won't even go near him when the babe's sick.'

'Myles is too old to be a father-figure, Florence.' Elizabeth reached for the butter.

'Isn't that what I just said? Why don't you latch on to this Logan guy, Elizabeth? Jeremy sure likes him. I told you to marry him the first time he came, remember?'

'Florence, quit while you're ahead.' Elizabeth picked up Jeremy's breakfast and went out on to the terrace.

Grady looked up from a line of toy soldiers and said cheerfully, 'Good morning, my lovely Elizabeth.'

'I am not your lovely anything.' She propped Jeremy up with pillows. 'There you go, Tiger. Take it easy at first to be sure you don't have any nasty chicken pox in your throat.'

'Could I have?'

'Probably not,' Grady advised. 'They keep that as a special treat for people who aren't smart enough to have them as kids. No—' he said to Elizabeth. 'You don't look your very best this morning. But by tomorrow you'll be back to beautiful again. I'm counting on it.'

'Does that mean if I turned into a hag overnight you wouldn't want to marry me?'

Jeremy's eyes rounded.

Grady grinned. 'I think you just made an announcement, Betsy.'

'Are you going to marry Grady, Mom?'

'No, I'm not. Now drink your breakfast.'

'I'm not hungry.'

'He must be sick,' Grady said.

'Why aren't you going to marry him? He's nice.' Jeremy reluctantly tipped up the glass.

'My very question,' Grady added. 'Why not? I'm nice.'

Elizabeth looked from one to the other. 'I ought to shoot the pair of you,' she announced finally. 'But since you seem to find such joy in each other's company, I'll leave you to it. Have a nice day. I'll tell Florence to bring your lunch out. And possibly your dinner too.' She marched across the terrace.

'I think she's mad at us,' Grady hazarded.

Jeremy set his glass down and started to shred his toast. 'Are you going to be my stepfather?' He looked worried, as if, on reflection, he had changed his mind.

'Your mother says not.' Grady studied the child for a moment and added casually, 'Would you mind?'

'No. . .'

'No . . . but what?'

Jeremy ducked his head and said softly, 'But I'd rather my father came back.'

After a moment, Grady asked, 'Do you remember your father?'

'No.'

'Then how do you know you'd like it if he came back? It seems to me he must have been a nasty person to walk out on you and your mother.'

Jeremy doubled up his fists. 'Don't you say that about my father! Take it back!'

'Okay, okay. I'll take it back—your father was a super guy.'

Jeremy had dissolved into tears. He was huddled into a pathetic heap in the chair.

Grady muttered, 'It seems like she could at least tell you the truth,' and picked the child up. Jeremy turned his face into Grady's shoulder.

Finally his sobs had died down to an occasional hiccup. When he spoke, his voice was so soft that Grady had to bend his head to hear. 'Was my father really a super guy?'

Grady answered with another question. 'Hasn't your mother told you anything about him?'

Jeremy shook his head. 'I ask and ask. She's still mad at him, like she's still mad at Uncle Rick for dying.'

'What?'

Jeremy nodded his head vigorously. 'She is—really. I heard her tell Florence. She's mad because he was all the family she had, except for Great-Grandfather, and he doesn't really count.' He added hastily, 'She knows Uncle Rick didn't die on purpose, but still. . .'

'All the family she had?'

'Yeah. Their mom and dad died when they were little, and Great-Grandfather took care of them. Then. . .'

'Myles really is her grandfather.' Then, approaching the subject delicately, 'Why does everybody call your mother Mrs Englin? She's really Miss Englin, isn't she?'

Troubled blue eyes looked up at him. 'I don't know.' Then, eager to be helpful, 'I remember something she told Florence about my father once.'

'Eavesdropping again?' Grady asked wryly.

'She said he was unhappy. She said he was a sad . . . a sad . . .'

Comprehension dawned in Grady's eyes. 'A sadist?'

'Yeah, that's it. But why was he sad?'

'I . . . don't think that's quite what she meant, Jeremy.'

'Oh. I don't understand why she divorced him because he was sad. That's why she took back her real name. I don't even know what his name was.' The big eyes started to fill with tears again. Jeremy dashed them away. 'I don't cry very often,' he said defensively.

Grady settled the child more comfortably on his lap. 'The world would be a better place if all of us cried more and punched less,' he said. He leaned his cheek against the soft blond hair and thought about it. After a few minutes, he said, 'Do you suppose we could pretend, you and I?'

'Pretend what?'

'I could pretend that you're really my son, and you could pretend that I'm really your father.'

'What good would that do?' Jeremy scoffed. 'She said she isn't going to marry you.'

'She'll change her mind,' Grady promised. 'She will most definitely change her mind.' He set Jeremy back into the lounge chair. 'Now, let's talk about something else—something fun.'

'Let's play cards.' Jeremy scrabbled in the bucket till he found a ragged pack.

'Are you sure they're all there? What shall we play?'

'War. Mom plays that with me sometimes when I'm sick. And Florence too. She tries to teach me solitaire games though, like Great-Grandfather plays. Do you know how to play War?'

'Yes, Jeremy. I, too, was once a small boy.' Grady stacked his cards neatly and flipped the first one over. 'Are you sick a lot?' He pushed the card over beside Jeremy's which had won the trick.

'It seems like always. Mom says I've got a lot of catching up to do.'

Grady took the next trick. 'What do you mean, a lot of catching up to do?' he asked idly.

'I was born too soon. She says the reason I'm so small for my age and always sick is that I wasn't ready to be born.' He flipped a card. 'War!' he shouted and put three cards face down and another was turned up.

Grady sat frozen. 'How much too soon were you born?'

'A lot. Aren't you going to put your cards down?'

'Sure.' Grady automatically laid out his cards.

'My jack beats your five!' Jeremy said gleefully, and swept the cards up. 'And I got a king of yours, too. I'm going to beat you, Grady!'

'Your birthday is in January, isn't it, Jeremy?'

'Yeah. The twenty-eighth. Turn a card up!'

Grady did. 'When were you supposed to be born?'

'I don't know. Who cares? But I only weighed three and a half pounds. That trick's yours.'

'I rather think it is,' Grady mused. 'Jeremy, do you think we could finish this a little later? I just thought of something I have to talk to your mother about.' He tousled the blond head. 'I'll be back as soon as I can.'

CHAPTER ELEVEN

ELIZABETH paced her room, feeling like a caged animal. It was too early to go downstairs to her office. She didn't dare go into the living room because Myles would be sure to show up, and if his eyebrows went any higher today Elizabeth wasn't sure she could maintain a ladylike pose. She had been driven out of the kitchen once by Florence's sense of humour—proof that the woman was cracked, Elizabeth thought bitterly, for what normal person would see humour in this!—and if she went within shouting distance of the terrace she'd have Grady nagging at her again, and probably Jeremy as well.

It just wasn't fair that Jeremy had gone over to the enemy camp, she told herself. Everybody was conspiring against her. Even Jared must have suspected what his brother had in mind, or he wouldn't have said some of the things he had at lunch yesterday. Myles was in favour; so were Whit and Helene; Florence thought it was a splendid idea—it just wasn't fair for Elizabeth to have to be the only one to hold out.

So why was she holding out?

She walked across to the window, stared out over the lake, and allowed herself a brief, heady view of what life would be like if she married Grady. It wasn't the money that mattered, she told herself, or the social position. She had had both of those all of her life. It was that controlled energy that seeped from him, that sense of being a spring tightly wound and ready to slip from control. There would never be a dull moment.

He had already stirred up her quiet backwater of a life so that it would take a long time to recede into calmness. If she married him, she would never know another instant of peace, and she'd love every moment of it, because Grady would make living exciting—as he had once before.

She stared at the deep blue water of Lake Michigan and admitted to herself what her heart had been trying to say for ten days. She had never got over their love affair that summer; no matter how hard she had tried to tell herself over the past five years that it was only infatuation, her heart had remained faithful. Faithful to a man who had walked out on her, she reminded herself.

Tom Bradford was right, she admitted. She was different when Grady was around. She was a woman in love, and women in love didn't care about façades and cool sophistication. Whether Grady stayed in Chicago or went to the far side of the globe, there would never be anyone else.

Why not marry him? she asked herself. He wanted her, and as he had told her so firmly, what he wanted, he got. She sighed and went to take her shower. What good was a marriage that wasn't built from love on both sides? In the cold light of day she could not forget Grady's statement that if he married her he would never love her, never be willing for her to have that hold over him. Without love, what kind of a marriage could it be?

'No kind at all,' she told herself firmly and got under the shower. As long as Grady persisted in believing her the sort of social climber and gold-digger who would do anything for money or position, he couldn't love her as she needed to be loved. She fleetingly thought about trying to convince him that she wasn't what he thought she was. But that thought swirled down the drain with the scented soap bubbles; he would never believe her, because she had done too convincing a job when she had been trying to protect herself from him.

She stood under the cool spray for a long time, letting the water soothe away the ache in her back and the tightness in her muscles. Finally, she reluctantly shut the taps off. If she stayed in the shower any longer, she'd turn into a prune.

She put on a peach-coloured suit with a bright blouse in turquoise and peach. It reflected some badly-needed colour into her cheeks. She brushed her hair up into a twist and applied make-up with a hand that was none too steady.

The smell of pecan rolls drifted from the kitchen as she passed, and Elizabeth wavered. But it wasn't worth facing Florence again. The woman was shrewd; she would have little trouble diagnosing Elizabeth's problem. Let Grady and Jeremy enjoy the pecan rolls. By evening, she would have herself under control again.

The door of Tom's office was open. 'You're supposed to be taking the weekend off,' she said, pausing in the doorway.

Tom looked up and smiled. '*You* can take the weekend off,' he said. It's called delegating authority. I haven't quite learned the skill yet. And why are you here at this hour?'

'I'm just hoping that an early start will make the day go quicker. What's the problem?' Elizabeth sat down in the comfortable chair next to his desk.

'This convention, still. I vote that if they want to come back next year, we tell them we're full.'

'My vote lies with yours—but we are still running a hotel. However, I doubt they'll be back.'

'Jill said you had real fun yesterday.' He was looking through a folder as he spoke, and Elizabeth thought he didn't even realise how he'd spoken the girl's name. Maybe that was going to work out after all. At least, thank heaven, it looked as if Tom wasn't going to waste time mourning for Elizabeth. It would have made a difficult working situation if he had.

'Why don't you come on into my office?' she suggested.

'I have a couple of matters I want you to handle first thing Monday morning, and since you're here. . .'

Tom groaned. 'Why do you think I came in at this unreasonable hour? Nobody expects you to be anywhere on the floor before ten.' But he followed her good-naturedly.

Elizabeth pushed her office door open and went in, talking over her shoulder to Tom.

'It's about time you got here,' Grady said. He was lounging in a chair next to her window, looking very much at ease.

'Call security, Tom. I want this guy out of here right now.'

'Don't do it, Tom,' Grady advised. 'She'll change her mind.'

'It's bad enough that I have to put up with you living one floor above me and insinuating yourself into Myles' company at every opportunity. I will not allow you to make yourself at home in my office. Now go away, or I'll have you thrown out.'

He got lazily to his feet. 'You have a very unhappy little boy upstairs, Betsy. A little boy who desperately wants to know the truth about his father.'

'Jeremy is my son, he's none of your business, and this is not the time I choose to talk about him.'

'But it's the time I choose. When are you going to tell him, Betsy? When are you going to answer his questions?'

She threw her handbag on to her desk. 'What do you want me to tell him? That his father was a cruel. . .'

Grady laughed. 'If you're going to spin me the tale about the sadist you were briefly married to, don't bother. I haven't heard it all, but already I don't believe it.'

Tom took a step forward. Calling the security guards was forgotten. 'Are you saying Elizabeth is a liar?'

'All the way, Bradford. For the best of reasons, of course—or at least she thinks they are. She didn't tell you the truth either, I presume. It's a nice story, actually—I think I have all of the main points. She married a man who hurt her so badly she couldn't bear to keep his name, even when she found out she was pregnant. It must have made it easier than admitting Jeremy was illegitimate.'

'Is this true, Elizabeth?' Tom demanded.

She nodded. 'Rick and I cooked it up. Alan McConnell did the paperwork.' Green eyes pleaded with him for understanding. 'Myles had just had a heart attack. It would have killed him to know that Jeremy wasn't legitimate.'

'He preferred to think you'd been through hell?' Grady asked unbelievingly.'

'He was sick. The scandal. . .'

'Oh, yes, the scandal. Why didn't you just have a quiet abortion, Betsy? Then no one would ever have known.'

'I couldn't.' Her voice was soft, tormented. She turned away. 'Get him out of here, Tom, please.'

'Oh, I'm going, if you insist.' But Grady stopped at the door.

'How do you know all of this, Logan?' Tom demanded.

Grady ignored him. 'Would you like to know what I'm going to do now, Betsy?'

'What?' Elizabeth's voice was a fearful whisper.

'I'm going to go out into the middle of the main lobby and call a press conference. And then I'm going to take all of those nice, news-hungry reporters up to your apartment and introduce them to—my son.'

'No!'

'Your son?' Tom asked disbelievingly. 'Jeremy?'

'Jeremy,' Grady repeated flatly. He turned to Elizabeth. 'That's the choice you've got, Betsy. Either we hash it out here—without Bradford—or I'll spread it all over the gossip columns. I might even sue you for custody. That would make a nice splash.'

Elizabeth sat down in the nearest chair. 'Tom, I think you'd better go,' she said finally.

'I was certain you'd see it my way,' Grady said cheerfully. He ushered an open-mouthed Tom to the door. 'By the way, I'm positive Elizabeth would appreciate it if all this went no further,' he pointed out, and closed the door before Tom could find an answer.

Grady stood for an instant, his hands braced against the door. When he turned to face her, his expression had changed. 'You told me once that you could find a couple of doctors who would swear that Jeremy was born prematurely. Of course you could, Betsy—they'd just be telling the truth. He was three months premature.'

'Not quite that much.' Her voice was listless. She supposed she should have realised that this was inevitable.

'When are you going to tell our son about his father?'

Anger boiled up in her. She jumped up, her despair forgotten. 'Right now,' she stormed. 'I'm going to tell him all about you—the spoiled darling of a wealthy family who didn't even care enough about me to bother to find out what I really was. You wanted me to be unsuitable because you needed an excuse to break away from your father. Did you ever wonder what happened to me? Did it ever cross your mind that there could have been a child? Is that what I'm supposed to tell my son about the man he idolises—the man he's created in his own mind?'

He seized her arms. 'No. You tell him about the man who loved you so much that he gave up his inheritance for you and started over to build something of his own to give you. I built it all from nothing, Betsy—I built it for you.'

'I would have settled for a phone call,' she said bitterly, and tried to turn away.

He wouldn't let go of her. 'I should have called right away. I was afraid to. I was afraid that as soon as you found out I was out of a job that you wouldn't have anything to do with me. I didn't want to find out if it was me you cared about, or only the Logan Banks. So I waited till I had a start. It wasn't much, and then when I called, you were gone. The manager would say only that you'd left suddenly—an illness in the family, he thought.'

'Myles' heart attack. But that was weeks, Grady! I thought you'd caved in to pressure, that you'd agreed not to see me again.'

'Whit wanted me to. You sounded like a fortune-hunter. That's why I quit. I wanted to come back and look for myself, but I couldn't leave. If I had, I'd not only have lost what little I had, but I'd have bankrupted Jared too. By the time I could leave, the inn had burned—the records were gone. Then we couldn't even find the other girls who had worked there that summer. The private investigators struck out everywhere looking for Betsy Ames.'

He had looked for her? He had waited for her? 'Ames was my mother's name,' she said softly, hardly knowing what words she used. 'Myles thought I was spending the summer with friends. He'd have killed me if he'd known I was working for the competition. He wouldn't believe that I really wanted to run the Englin. I was trying to prove to him I could do it.' She sighed. 'Then he got sick, and I didn't have to prove anything.'

Grady drew a deep breath. 'After a while I even contacted my father. I thought perhaps you'd tried to reach me. He said no, there'd been no word. I called him a liar, Betsy—my own father.'

'I thought you'd decided the money was more important than I was, and I still had some pride, Grady. If Betsy Ames wasn't good enough for you, then Elizabeth Englin wasn't either.'

He let her go and walked across the room, the repressed energy driving him on. 'I waited five years. I thought something must have happened to you—I couldn't bring myself to believe that you just didn't care, or that you didn't want to have anything to do with me. Then I called my father and told him that building a wall down the middle of a family was a darn stupid way to live. He told me to come home. And he suggested I come out here.' He started to laugh. 'When I saw you again, and thought you had used Rick to make your way up the ladder, it sickened me. For about the first ten minutes. After that—' He shook his head. 'I knew I had to have you. It didn't matter what you'd done, even if you'd picked up the next available man after I went out of your life. Even if there'd been a man before me, one you'd cared enough about to have his child. I just knew I had to have you.'

'You said you'd never fall in love with me.' Elizabeth's voice sounded unfamiliar to her own ears. She stared out of the window.

'I didn't care if you loved me. But I was afraid if you knew how much you meant to me, you'd use that.' He came across the room to her, and let one finger slide gently down her cheek. 'Betsy—I have to know. Why didn't you take the easy way out? Why didn't you have an abortion?'

She stared out over the lake, absently watching a white-sailed boat leaving the marina for the open water, as she searched for words. 'I thought about it. But I couldn't arbitrarily end a life that started in such innocent joy. And then one night I realised that as long as I had the baby I'd have part of you—even if I never saw you again.' She turned to look at him. 'He is like you, Grady.'

He nodded. 'I can see that now. I was too jealous to see it before.'

There was a short silence. Elizabeth, suddenly comprehending his uneasiness, said, 'I'm sorry. It's a great embarrassment for you, to find that you have a son who's five years old. I must have forgotten how I felt at first, wondering what people were saying about me. Perhaps I should have had an abortion—but I don't regret it,

Grady. I can't imagine a world that didn't have Jeremy in it.'

'Neither can I.'

She stumbled on, unhearing, her great green eyes full of tears, pleading for understanding. 'I don't want you to be hurt by it. No one needs to know, Grady, ever. Whit and Helene—I'll never tell them. Tom won't tell anyone, if I ask him not to.' She choked on a sob. 'You can see Jeremy if you want. I won't ask you to acknowledge him. . . I'll never tell him who his father is. . .'

'Won't you? I will.' He gave her a quick little shake. 'My lovely darling, don't you understand what you've done? I want to go and stand in the middle of Michigan Avenue and announce to anyone who will listen that my son is upstairs with the chicken pox. Betsy, will you marry me? Not because of Jeremy. Not for any reason other than because I love you.'

She brushed a lock of hair back from his forehead. 'Do you need to ask?'

He kissed her then, a long, lingering kiss that left them both trembling with unfulfilled desire. Then Grady set her firmly aside. 'It's a good thing we're in an office,' he mused, 'or I'd probably forget that there's a little unsettled matter waiting upstairs. I have a card game to finish with my son.'

EPILOGUE

THE bride wore her grandmother's dress, the best man was the proudest five-year-old in Chicago, the reception was the largest the Englin Hotel ever hosted. After the rice was thrown, the newlyweds gone, and the best man tucked in bed to dream of a happy future, the father of the groom and the grandfather of the bride retired to Myles' library to drink a toast to the absent couple.

'To our children—may they always be as happy as they were today,' Whit said, and raised his glass.

Myles drank, and asked pensively, 'Do you think we ever dare tell them that we figured it out a couple of years ago?'

Whit choked, laughed, and refilled his glass. 'Those two hotheads? No,' he advised. 'At least not till Jeremy's wedding day.' He held the glass high. 'To our grandson,' he said, with deep satisfaction.

LEIGH MICHAELS likes writing romance fiction spiced with humor and a dash of suspense and adventure. She holds a degree in journalism and teaches creative writing in Iowa. She and her husband, a photographer, have two children but include in their family a dog-pound mutt who thinks he's human and a Siamese "aristo-cat," both of whom have appeared in her books. When asked if her husband and children have also been characterized, the author pleads the Fifth Amendment.

The Grand Hotel is a prequel to *Touch not My Heart*, Harlequin Presents 876.

Books by Leigh Michaels

Don't miss any of our special offers. Write to us at the following address for information on our newest releases.

Harlequin Reader Service
901 Fuhrmann Blvd., P.O. Box 1397, Buffalo, NY 14240
Canadian address: P.O. Box 603,
Fort Erie, Ont. L2A 5X3

Can you keep a secret?

You can keep this one plus 4 free novels

Harlequin Presents

Coming Next Month

Available in August wherever paperback books are sold, or through Harlequin Reader Service:

In the U.S.
901 Fuhrmann Blvd.
P.O. Box 1397
Buffalo, N.Y. 14240-1397

In Canada
P.O. Box 603
Fort Erie, Ontario
L2A 5X3

In August
Harlequin celebrates

The 1000th Presents

Passionate Relationship

by
Penny Jordan

Harlequin Presents,
still and always the No. 1 romance
series in the world!

Available wherever paperback books are sold.

PR1000

ATTRACTIVE, SPACE SAVING BOOK RACK

Display your most prized novels on this handsome and sturdy book rack. The hand-rubbed walnut finish will blend into your library decor with quiet elegance, providing a practical organizer for your favorite hard-or soft-covered books.

Only $9.95

Approximately 16" x 8" when assembled

Assembles in seconds!

To order, rush your name, address and zip code, along with a check or money order for $10.70* ($9.95 plus 75¢ postage and handling) payable to *Harlequin Reader Service*:

Harlequin Reader Service
Book Rack Offer
901 Fuhrmann Blvd.
P.O. Box 1396
Buffalo, NY 14269-1396

Offer not available in Canada.

BKR-1A

*New York and Iowa residents add appropriate sales tax.

Sarah

MAURA SEGER

Sarah wanted desperately to escape the clutches of her cruel father.
Philip needed a mother for his son, a mistress for his plantation.
It was a marriage of convenience.
Then it happened. The love they had tried to deny suddenly became a
blissful reality... only to be challenged by life's hardships and brutal
misfortunes.

JULIE ELLIS

**author of the bestselling
Rich Is Best rivals the likes of
Judith Krantz and Belva Plain with**

THE ONLY SIN

It sweeps through the glamorous cities of Paris, London, New York and Hollywood. It captures life at the turn of the century and moves to the present day. *The Only Sin* is the triumphant story of Lilli Landau's rise to power, wealth and international fame in the sensational fast-paced world of cosmetics.

**For the millions who can't read
Give the Gift of Literacy**

One out of five adults in North America
cannot read or write well enough
to fill out a job application
or understand the directions on a bottle of medicine.

**You can change all this by joining the fight
against illiteracy.**

For more information write to:
Contact, Box 81826, Lincoln, Neb. 68501
In the United States, call toll free: 800-228-3225

**The only degree you need
is a degree of caring**